Tales from the Southside

A collection of short stories, poetry and flash fiction
Compiled by Frank Chambers and Alex Meikle

Copyright © 2024

All rights reserved.

ISBN: 9798342034319

All rights reserved, including the right to reproduce this book, or any portion thereof in any form. No part of this book may be reproduced, transmitted, downloaded, reverse engineered, or stored, in any form or introduced into any information storage and retrieval system, in any form or by any means, electronic or mechanical without the express written permission of the authors.

Contents

THE OLD TRAM STOP	DIANE OSPREY	1
HOME BIRTH 4 GARTURK STREET	CHRISTINA MILARVIE QUARRELL	5
THE BOY WHO LIKED SHAKESPEARE	HENRY BUCHANAN	6
HOPE	ANNIE HEALY	20
YOU CAN'T TRUST ANYONE THESE DAYS	MAUREEN MYANT	22
A MIRACLE IN AUGUST	IAN DONALDSON	30
NO SHELTER FROM THE STORM	TRACEY MCBAIN	32
THE LINDEN BLOSSOM	SLAVA KONOVAL	44
INSIDE THE CIRCLE	FRANK CHAMBERS	45
MARIAN'S GHOSTS FAE LANGSIDE	IAN GOUDIE	52
RUDER FORMS SURVIVE	JONATHAN CHARLES NAPIER	53
GLORIA	DAVID STAKES	63
A DAY AT THE SEASIDE	ALEX MEIKLE	66
THE QUEEN OF THE SHAWS	LAURA MCPHERSON	75
SINCERITY IS JIGGERY-POKERY	HUGH V. MCLACHLAN	77
TARTAN DREAMS	ALAN GILLESPIE	87
LA SIGNORA SWEENEY	BARNEY MACFARLANE	88
THE ROUND	J D ALLAN	91
TOM	SANDY MCGIVEN	93
MUSINGS ON A MAT	GILLIAN BOOTH	98
TRIP TO SCOTLAND 2023 - SOUTHSIDE MEMORIES	DANIEL RITCHIE	100
MINI CONE	ELLIE NESS	106
A WALK IN THE PARK	KARMJIT BADESHA	107
THE SOU'SIDE SETTLER	SHIRLEY MACKIE	112
FINDING BLACKIE MCGINLAY	LESLEY O'BRIEN	116
BATTLEFIELD - A TABLEAUX	BORIS PICHOTKA	125
MOTHER'S BLESSINGS	ELIZABETH R. ETHERIDGE	127
GETTING FIT	MARCO GIANNASI	131
LIES	IAIN BAIN	133
250 BATTLEFIELD ROAD	CHRISTINA MILARVIE QUARRELL	138
MAYFAIR MAYHEM	V MCKENNA	139
CORPORAL EDWARD FERRIE	TRACEY MCBAIN	143
FAME AND MUSIC	WILLIE BROWN	144
THE GRANARY, 1985	DEBORAH PORTILLA	148
YAWN BONNIE BANKS	BARNEY MACFARLANE	150
FULL CIRCLE	ROSALYN BARCLAY	151
ODE TO THE CAIRNS	STEPHEN TIGGERDINE	156

The Old Tram Stop by Diane Osprey

Chantelle stands at the lights beside the Co-op, just as Sam had told her. Crossing the road, she thinks, what the fuck. I'd said a fancy pizza gaff, what's this place. It's like a dodgy wedding cake, how the fuck do you get in?

Sam waits inside. Hope this hits the mark. She'd said a nice Italian posh place, surprise me. The door opens, of sorts, he sees someone struggling to work the old-fashioned wooden swing doors. It's her.

Chantelle enters. Sam waves her over. While doing so, he knocks over half the table contents, solid cutlery crashing to the floor. "Christ, these pokey tables, never enough room."

"Fuck's sake man. This place is like an old folks' living room on heat. You're stuck in the middle of a roundabout or something, everyone staring at you. Call this a table for two. You'd be lucky if it can fit wan pizza on it."

"Did you find the place okay then, Chantelle?"

She stares around, clocking all the old pictures. In her sarcastic tone, which hides all sorts, she snorts, "This place is like the bog on the outside, all shiny. Whit's that aw aboot, bathroom tiles on the outside. Would've been better if you'd said the cake in the middle of the road. Thought it was pizza wae you, no half of Battlefield joining us. Do they call it 'Rest' because it's where all the old folk end up. I mean it's like the Queen Vic or something, aw these old picture things on the walls."

"It's an Italian bistro Chantelle. They do a great pre-theatre deal." Just as Sam launches into his usual calm the situation down chat, a waiter arrives, all in his whites. He speaks with a thick Italian accent. Sam orders 2 cokes and asks the waiter to give them a few minutes to decide.

"I cannae understand a fucking thing he's saying."

"They employ a lot of Italian staff. Look at the menu."

Chantelle's eyes dart all over the menu. She munches at her already stubby worn-out nails. Sam is all too aware that she will struggle with both reading and knowing the food.

"Do you need a hand with any of the dishes? Sometimes it can be confusing."

"Naw, I'm no fucking stupid. I just want pizza."

"How about I surprise you, pizza and some other stuff too. Birthday treat and all."

"If you want." This was a typical default response for Chantelle.

Sam hands her a gift bag, then disappears to the bar and puts in the order. He glances back at her, catching her doing likewise. When she thinks it's safe, she rips open the card and gift bag. Her eyes are wide with delight, which she quickly hides as Sam returns.

"That okay? Thought that I would let you buy some of that tatt you like. Primark does it all."

"Aye, ah suppose so. Ta." Chantelle had never been given anything like a £100 voucher.

"We'll share two starters and then two mains. You can have the pudding. Ah'm no really into sweet stuff."

A bruschetta and pate arrive. Sam explains the dishes.

"Ah know. Ah'm no thick." Chantelle dives in, pauses, then waits to watch Sam execute the food.

"Delicious," he says, "what do you think?"

"Aw right, I suppose. Don't really like veggies."

A huge pizza arrives and a plate of mussels. Chantelle continues to look nonchalant.

"You okay to share?"

"Aye, but I think they've forgot to take them shell things aff."

"Oh, sometimes they do, sometimes they don't." Sam often gives her a get out. "I love picking them out of the shells and stuffing the bread into the dip."

It doesn't take much for her to get where this is going and she tears in, appearing ravenous. Sam got around two or three mussels. Rather than ask what was on the pizza, Chantelle starts to rip at it with her hands. Seeing Sam use his cutlery, she quickly adapts to his likewise norms.

"This mince is great."

"Yes, they mix it up a bit. It's often haggis." Sam pretends to study the taste. "Yip, haggis this time."

Chantelle blandly states, "Aye, ah pure love haggis me."

"Yeah, the caramelised onions really add to it, don't they."

"If you think so. Ah'm no bothered." As Chantelle wolfs down every last morsel that was the pizza.

"There's that dodgy waiter. Whit's he doing?" Chantelle then finds herself being serenaded by said dodgy waiter. She recognised the tune but not the words. He lights a candle and blasts out an Italian version of the birthday tune. Sam fondly looks on, trying so hard not to smile too much, from cheek to cheek.

"Fuck's sake, whit's that aw aboot? A pure riddy."

Sam could tell that she was touched. He was all too aware that birthdays never really existed for Chantelle, much the same with most milestone moments. She'd never gotten gifts. Any money was spent on her mother's habit. This dinner was to celebrate both Chantelle's 17th birthday, and she and Sam working together for 6 months. Of all his caseload, he felt a real tear at his heart for Chantelle. Her life had simply been shit, then social services called. Some might say her life is still shit.

"This is an unusual type of cake, Chantelle. It has got a really funny name. It's called Tiramisu, a traditional Italian dessert. I guess a bit like trifle for us."

Chantelle, true to form, without hesitation, scoffs the lot.

Sam settles up the bill and they head outside.

"I hope that was okay."

"Aye aw right, if you like that sort of thing. Whit's the place called again?"

"The Battlefield Rest. It used to be an old tram stop, that's why it's kind of in the middle of the road. You were spot on about that, Chantelle."

She beamed. Chantelle loved the recognition, she got so little in life.

"Ah'm aff now." She quickly tries to say something nice but finds it so hard to do. She heads to the crossing and turns.

"Sam?"

"Yeah."

"Thanks. Ah've never had Italian cake before. Will I see you next week?" Her guard let down.

"Of course. I'll ring you on Monday for our weekly phone check-in and you can let me know where you want to meet, always Thursday at 5. If anything crops up, call me. Remember Chantelle anytime, day or night."

She turns and leaves smiling. Chantelle waits until she has turned the corner, opposite the library, feeling safe that Sam can't see her, she skips with delight. Thinking that was pure banging. Running over in her head the dinner plates and tastes, none of the like she has heard or seen before, and thinks to herself, AH PURE LUV ITALIAN STUFF.

Home Birth 4 Garturk Street by Christina Milarvie Quarrell

being a Soo Side born child
growing happily into
a traditional build
not a wee thin kind

I find comfort
in the Scottish homily
appreciated by my
well put together
sisters and relations

"better tae huv the weight
tae lose if yir noo weel"

my maternal granny
often loudly stated
wisdom handed down
from our ancestors
(some who ate grass)

survival their sacred mission.

The Boy who liked Shakespeare by Henry Buchanan

Key chapters of your life are a watershed, pushing you onto one path and not another. For Johnsey Kelvin the watershed began early in secondary school when his Maths teacher was off, and the class got a student replacement for a few days. Johnsey liked it right away. Rather than commencing the lesson with a blackboard example of a new type of equation followed by interminable practice, a young bearded fellow kicked off with the statement that "mathematics is fun," went on about the ancient Greeks and then got into the history of the subject.

"Maths is beautiful," the guy declared in exuberant tones, pointing to the beautiful spring morning outside. On the blackboard he plotted an elegant tangent function graph in its positive and negative aspects and explained infinity. He asked them if they thought that maths was a real science. If anyone knew the square root of negative 1. What is an "imaginary number"? What is zero? All of this caused consternation amongst James Kearney and his crowd of budding prefects at the front of the class who sat with their textbooks at-the-ready to resume the normal course of instruction, although the

Oxbridge hopefuls and one or two of the girls were displaying some enthusiasm.

The new teacher then got onto non-Euclidean geometry and asked everyone to consider whether parallel lines could meet in infinity—but he was cut short by grumbles from the front and by Kearney chucking down his pen in annoyance. To Johnsey's great disappointment, the teacher abandoned his lecture, quickly scribbled a textbook equation and its solution on the blackboard and told the class to do the rest of the exercises.

Johnsey did two or three equations before being struck motionless by the brilliant low-angled morning sun streaming into the classroom and by the beautiful patterns of light and shade outside. His thoughts went into slow motion and were speeding up at the same time. He was thinking about life, the universe and everything. He began seeing himself from the outside, seeing himself not being like the others. His thoughts fixed on Kearney's crowd who had buried their heads in their textbooks and jotters without once looking up. They were happy to be regimented, happy to torture themselves this fine morning with ever more complex quadratic equations. They did not want to think about maths, they only wanted a good grade. School, university, work—their lives were already mapped out like one of those graphs on the blackboard. They would become well-paid servants of the system and were already jostling for position.

Towards the end of the lesson, he raised his hand to find out more from the teacher, but there were tuts of disapproval from Prentice at the front. So he spent the last couple of minutes listening to his friends Hub and Noddy whispering Marx Brothers jokes.

That was the day Johnsey resolved not to do any more homework and not to study towards a university place.

II

Johnsey allowed himself to drop down a dozen places in all his subjects and avoided anything he found boring. But the following spring, with the appearance of the first low-angled rays of the sun, his interest in school things was revived. It happened in Miss MacDonald's English class when they were reading out *Julius Caesar,* and shafts of sunlight were streaming into the classroom with a brilliant whiteness. She was explaining Shakespeare's "iambic pentameter" verse and why the words are set down as poetry on the page. Ten syllables to the line, five weak stresses alternate with five strong stresses, you almost sing the line, *tee-tum, tee-tum, tee-tum, tee-tum, tee-tum.* This had evolved from ancient Greece when music and maths were the same.

What? Music and maths the same! Johnsey had never suspected such hidden depths in writing and wanted to find out more. He paid more attention in class and Miss MacDonald said he should read out the part of Calpurnia in *Julius Caesar* because of his high voice and because boys played female roles on the Elizabethan stage. So Johnsey didn't mind being sissyish—liking Shakespeare and reading a female part—if it meant discovering the mysteries of writing. He also had a vague intuition that Shakespeare was used by the system to keep the poor people down, but this was also intriguing.

On the last Saturday of the Easter break he sat down to read the second act of *Julius Caesar.* He became so engrossed that he read the play right through till the end and even forgot to go through to the living room to watch the football highlights on

TV with his father. He was exhilarated and wanted more Shakespeare. He pulled out Miss MacDonald's twenty-questions worksheet from his schoolbag. *Julius Caesar* is set in 1) Carthage, 2) Athens, 3) Rome. He did the first eight or nine questions.

Since childhood Shakespeare had been a magic name, a special and mysterious realm the fascination of which he was yet to understand. Johnsey turned to the notes in his *Junior School Edition* and learned that virtually nothing was known about William Shakespeare. Books at home were sparse, but he went to his brother's twelve-volume *Encyclopaedia* and picked up on the word "puzzle." He would ask the teacher about this.

III

On the Monday, waves of anxiety and excitement rippled through the English class. Miss MacDonald had remained in Paris after the Easter break—the girls were speculating on a romantic intrigue—and Mr Mills, department head, would take them for the next few weeks. Opinions were divided on this development. Kearney and the budding prefects worried that her tried-and-tested method of answering twenty questions and memorising ten quotations would be discarded, while the Oxbridge hopefuls seemed to welcome Mr Mills' lecturing style which was normally reserved for the senior pupils.

Mr Mills cut a maverick figure in the school; sporting a light green tweed jacket with leather elbow patches, he looked every inch the university professor. Those privy to staff room gossip told how he had been a brilliant scholar at Cambridge before being sent down for some misdemeanour or other. He had read all thirty-six Shakespeare plays. He had once published an article on Renaissance Literature in a prestigious journal, and only recently, when Women's Lib was impressing itself upon everyone else, he had printed a satirical burlesque in rhyming couplets in a literary magazine.

Mr Mills arrived and, far from exploding into lectures, had rather demurely proceeded with *Julius Caesar* in the normal way—they would read out the parts and sometimes make a note of key quotations. Johnsey was getting much more out of the play this time. He became engrossed again and began to understand much more. But after Caesar was assassinated, try as he might he could not refrain from giggling on picking up on Shakespeare's humour when Brutus and Cassius—in lines being read out by Kearney and Prentice no less—say that they had done Caesar a favour by shortening his time of "fearing death."

Mr Mills, distracted by Johnsey's giggles, looked over to him and Johnsey immediately raised his hand.

"Who was Shakespeare, sir?" Johnsey blurted out, self-conscious about having broken the rhythm of the lesson.

"Who was Shakespeare?" Mr Mills repeated, suddenly livening up. "An excellent question, good sir. How could the glovemaker's son from Stratford with no university education have produced the finest literature in the English language? Knowing obscure books in French and Italian, knowing Virgil and Ovid in Latin? Put down your pens and pencils, my young scholars," he directed, eyes screwing to a slant to access some deep inner space and leaving his chair to saunter about the floor of the classroom.

In the front rows, the budding prefects were turning round to stare out Johnsey who always sat in the middle of the room with Hub and Noddy. Worse, as he reddened and gulped, Prentice grimaced and shook his head, while Kearney, the 3rd year sports captain and unofficial leader of the class, even ventured to punch his palm with his fist with an onomatopoetic smack.

Mr Mills broke out of his trance. "Who was Shakespeare?" he repeated. "This is a question that has perplexed a small minority of scholars for more than a hundred years. Shakespeare wasn't Shakespeare, they say, we know virtually nothing about this man. Stratford Will, they say, just worked for the theatre company and the plays were actually written by the philosopher, essayist and scientist, Sir Francis Bacon!"

For the rest of the lesson, Mr Mills lectured them on the background to *Julius Caesar*. He implored them to find out about what was happening in England at the time of the play in 1599. A time when Queen Elizabeth the First was old and childless but refused to name an heir to the throne, a time when King James of Scotland sought succession to her crown and was supported by the disgraced Earl of Essex who desperately wanted power and might stop at nothing. "Some see this story in the play and whoever wrote it seems to have been an aristocrat privy to court intrigues. Of course, playing for such high stakes made it necessary for the writer to dissemble."

"Dissemble?" Someone asked what this meant.

"Dissemblance is where you make out that something wasn't you," Mills replied instantly, "of giving the appearance of something being otherwise," and explained it in many different ways. When the bell rang for the end of class, he concluded: "To believe it or not to believe it—that is the question!"

For homework, he informed everyone that since he dissented from rote learning methods they should instead go to the library and find two or three points of interest in *Julius Caesar*.

IV

Mr Mills commenced the English class the next day by analysing Mark Antony's famous speech after Caesar's assassination, "Friends, Romans, countrymen, lend me your ears," which he read out himself. He asked them to consider Mark Antony's rhetorical techniques. Look how Antony says he has come "to bury Caesar, not to praise him," but cleverly uses language to turn the plebeians against the conspirators. Look how Antony refutes Brutus' claim that Caesar was "ambitious" through his story of Caesar refusing the emperor's crown three times. Look how Antony's repetition of "Brutus is an honourable man" implies the opposite. Mr Mills went on in this vein for more than twenty minutes and delivered a thorough analysis of the speech. He wound down and said, "Any questions?"

To the grumbles of Kearney and company, who would have liked to have made even more notes, Johnsey asked Mr Mills if Shakespeare was really the lover of Queen Elizabeth.

"No," he laughed, "this is preposterous because Shakespeare the man was lower class. So even if Shakespeare was the writer of the plays, he couldn't have got anywhere near her. Yet to better understand *Julius Caesar*, the queen does become part of the equation. Think about the assassination. Is this Rome in 31BC—or London in 1599 when the play was written and when there was a brewing conspiracy against Queen Elizabeth by the Earl of Essex who would later get his head chopped off."

The Oxbridge hopefuls were intrigued, as were Gwen Campbell, Elaine Mackie and Nora May. Kearney and his crowd were annoyed and refused to engage, while Smiddy and Thommo at the back stretched out and kicked Johnsey's seat a few times.

By now, Mr Mills had launched into one of his lectures and was once again sauntering about the classroom floor. But he was eventually cut short by Kearney.

"Sir, sir," he said respectfully, "some of us are falling behind in English and do not have time for secondary information on Shakespeare." Kearney had even procured an official sheet on examination guidelines and marking instructions and read bits of it out.

Mills was very sympathetic and said he would do his best to stick to more routine material, if they so wished. He asked the class to form small groups to discuss Mark Antony's speech. But someone soon wound him up again by rather naughtily asking whether they should visit the Shakespeare Birthplace in Stratford. For the remaining few minutes, Mills ranted against the idea. Stratford was all about money and power. Their professors were out for a career and were not real critics. They were not original thinkers. They were parrots who squawk off textbooks and for whom Shakespeare was a religion and Stratford a holy shrine. They were—

The bell rang.

"English?" Kearney whined as he stomped towards the door followed by his troupe, "it's more like the effing Marx Brothers in here," projecting his words to the back of the classroom.

V

Johnsey knew that he had fallen from grace, that he had lost the protection of the budding prefects who had hitherto kept order. At one time, if he had toed the line, he could have become a lesser member of their group—though not of course the goofs and freaks he hung around with. A phrase from *Julius Caesar*, "Beware the Ides of March," kept intruding into his thoughts. The attack came on the day of the annual Sports afternoon. With the exception of those bent on athletic achievement—Kearney and company were of course keen participants, being dead set on prefecture—the whole day was treated as a school holiday by the rest of the pupils, many of whom swarmed into Queen's Park. Johnsey went with Noddy and Hub.

Hub had wanted to try out a new technique for the high jump and had brought along a length of string to serve as the bar. And, *hooray*, his big brother had bought three bottles of cider and planked them in the bushes for afterwards. Hub told how he had been blown away when watching the Mexico Olympics and Dick Fosbury had run up and flipped backwards over the bar and won the gold medal. It was not allowed at the school sports because you would fall on sand, not on inflated cushions, but they were going to try it out. "Something to do with a lower centre of gravity" he enthused, "like the small scrum-half in rugby or small midfielders in football."

Down at the dense undergrowth, they took turns. Two held the string at almost head height while the third sailed over it backwards to land in the thick bushes on which they had piled their jumpers and jackets. They were surprised at the height they could jump. The "Fosbury Flop" it was called. They had a couple of jumps each, but soon the Park Keeper appeared blowing his whistle telling them to stop.

Next, they kicked a football around, Hub supplying the commentary. *Baxter does keepie-uppie against England at Wembley*.

Pele spins a shot, Lev Yashin changes direction in mid-air to save. George Best with an overhead kick. Goal!

To the left, just outside the park, the early spring sun struck the church spire at an inspiring angle as they sat down to their sandwiches around their pile of jumpers and jackets halfway up the hill. To the right, Gwen, Elaine and a crowd of girls had settled down, singing pop songs along with their transistor radio and messing around with their hockey sticks. After a few minutes Gwen came dancing by to give them some spare ice creams one of the mothers had dropped off.

"Tootsie-frootsie ica cream. It'sa no-bad," Noddy enthused in his Chico Marx accent.

Hub had retrieved the cider from the bushes and after the first bottle they were soon yattering away. Hub was reciting sketches from Monty Python's Flying Circus and the Marx Brothers' films. Noddy declaimed that "music is the message," said he was a hippie and that pot was good and raved on about counter-culture and someone called Malcolm X. Johnsey delighted in telling how he had asked Mr Mills again who Shakespeare was, whether Mills had got it all from books. No, he assured him, he had found the plays to be full of all kinds of genius and thought that the writer couldn't have contained this genius in just stage-plays and a few poems. He must have written more, much more, and Mills had wanted to read it. He found it in the writings of Bacon who wrote about everything. "Wow, what a gas, man!"

As they downed the second bottle, Hub got talking about a new TV series called Star Trek and then about some science fiction film where the twelve-year-olds were made leaders and presidents. Hub thought this was brilliant because children have to take in everything that's ever happened since the beginning of time and are therefore older than adults. They all got onto the puzzling ending to *2001: A Space Odyssey*. Johnsey told how the science teacher, Mr Ancaster, had explained that the obelisk thing appeared four times and symbolised stages of evolution from ape to man to spaceman to some higher stage of consciousness … but he lost concentration when out of the corner of his eye he spotted Smiddy, Thommo and a squad of six or seven others striding past them in a tight formation up the hill, discreetly passing bottles of El Dorado between them. To show off their splendid Arthur Black shirts they all had their jumpers tied around their waists like tunics—which made Johnsey think of the Roman legionnaires of two thousand years ago on this very patch of ground marching up to the fort on Camphill.

"El Dorado! El Dorado! Wine, wine, wine," the squad chanted as they marched up to the flagpole at the top of the hill to bevvy.

Halfway through the third bottle, the three became euphoric. Noddy told how he liked the *2001* director and loved *Spartacus* because of the slave revolt. And his film about atomic war, what's its name? He was joining the Ban the Bomb movement and had bought a pair of loons because hippies were cool. Spontaneously, he broke into song with the first verse of the "Ballad of Ho Chi Minh." He got up from the grass, pulled on his combat jacket and chanted "Ho, Ho, Ho Chi Minh! Ho, Ho, Ho Chi Minh!" and punched the air with his clenched fist.

"More protest music, *America* by The Nice," an elated Noddy ordered, and all three sang and pounded their imaginary electric organs like Keith Emerson.

De-de-de-de-de-de-dee-di-dah, de-de-de-de-de-dee-di-dah …

As they blasted out the best rock instrumental ever ever ever, Gwen, Elsbeth and the hockey girls looked on bemusedly. But Johnsey sobered slightly on observing that Smiddy, Thommo and their squad were now making their way back down the hill in between the two groups. He was humming the nursery rhyme "The Grand Old Duke of York" to himself in apprehension—but thankfully they passed by again down to the bottom of the hill.

They downed some more cider and were soon re-enacting the Ministry of Silly Walks sketch from Monty Python, passers-by stopping to look on. They strode around in all directions and performed the silliest walks imaginable—Noddy stealing the show with a semi-effeminate military march.

After they finished off the dregs of the cider, they started to knock the ball about again. But danger loomed. The squad was now neither up the hill nor down the hill but only halfway up—and fanning out towards them. "No, it's not like The Grand Old Duke of York," a slightly inebriated Johnsey sniggered to himself. He resigned himself to the fact that he was to be shortly duffed up, adopted a pose of indifference, and tried to detach himself from himself.

"Hey, it's the effing Marx Brothers," Smiddy announced rather jovially, making a beeline for Johnsey and motioning his henchmen forward.

"Goofy wee Johnsey!" Smiddy sneered, quickening towards him. "Freaks," Thommo yelled, darting in and feigning a punch but actually no more than telegraphing a kick to the balls which Johnsey easily palmed off with his hands. But he had stooped too low in doing so and on his blindside Smiddy floated in. His black Doc Marten boot—exquisitely laced and finely polished, a nice touch—rose from the grass with medium velocity and struck Johnsey smack in the face with a well-placed beauty of the instep. Had it been one-against-one, it would have been a not bad piece of athleticism, Johnsey thought. Another one sneaked in from behind and kneed him up the arse with moderate force, but his assailants were already making off in the direction of the girls when the Park Keeper appeared, sending shrill blasts of his whistle from the nearby path.

"A'm reportin youse aw tae the school," the Park-Keeper hollered to all and sundry.

Johnsey stood a bit dazed and was bleeding slightly from the nose—perhaps more than slightly—but already he began to muse on the symbolic nature of it all and how society worked.

"You okay?" his comrades asked after they had trudged up to the top of the hill below the flagpole.

Johnsey looked west to the pretty church spire for uplifting patterns of light and shade but there were none. "Och, the church spire is not so in*spir*ing now," he smirked, addressing the universe as much as his friends.

But then, just as they were moving off, in the low-angled rays of the early evening sun he caught a glimpse of the hazy gleam of the Glasgow University building jutting out nonchalantly on the distant hill beyond the church, proud and resplendent, bathed in mystique, as if beckoning him to come and play.

VI

The decision whether to involve the headmaster or the police was all but resolved the next morning with a message on the school noticeboard. *The South Side Academy would not tolerate truancy and drinking alcohol in Queen's Park*, it read, *boys drinking*

and fighting and making utter fools of themselves would be severely dealt with. Such vandals and hooligans would be immediately expelled and sent down to the Technical School to take courses in woodwork and joinery ...
Anyway, Johnsey owed it to Hub and Noddy to let the whole thing blow over.

Johnsey thought long and hard about all that had happened. He could never stop playing with his curiosity, *no*, that was impossible. But he would have to survive. From that day on he worked tirelessly on thoughts which could aid his survival, and which much later became refined into a secret motto: "Silence, dissemblance and invisibility."

On the Friday it was put out that Miss MacDonald was returning on Monday, and this would be their last class with Mr Mills. Mills went round everyone one by one and gave them essay plans to study for *Julius Caesar* for the forthcoming exam.

"Look," Mr Mills said when he got to Johnsey, "if you don't make the English class for Shakespeare next year, you can drop in on me. You can still do *Hamlet*." Then, just as Johnsey was taking in the beautiful patterns of light and shade outside, Mills produced an old tattered copy of *The Collected Works of William Shakespeare* and tossed it onto his desk. "Keep."

"*De omnibus dubitandum*," Mills said in a wise sort of tone. Johnsey, turfed out of Latin in his first year, knew not what this meant.

"Doubt all things," Mr Mills translated.

Hope by Annie Healy

I saw you again today, you are growing tall, beginning to look strong
I worried about you initially, I felt sure something could go wrong
Even on the coldest Battlefield days you continuously filled me with hope
Hope for a future for us, and planet earth now hanging by a very thin rope

I want to hold you and caress you and breathe in your scent
Your strength fills me up with sunshine, for now, our worst winter days have went.
Nobody else seems to see you quite the way I do
Your very presence does not even touch them, it's sad but it's true

People rushing past, hiding under umbrellas, some with dogs who continuously bark
Your little head peering through the wrought iron railings surrounding the beautiful Queens Park

You stand there bravely, raising your head up to any peep of sun and fighting off those April showers, you stand with pride among your peers, amidst a bed of flowers

Irrespective of the weather, you make the most of every day, you get stronger, more colourful, more animated, your sheer determination takes my breath away.

To watch you as you wave to me and yet barely level with my feet
You picked me, but I will never pick you my friend, your life is already too short and far too sweet
I will instead remember you forever and love you for as long as you remain
My beautiful yellow daffodil, everyone else's loss to your beauty, your sign of hope has certainly been my gain

You Can't Trust Anyone These Days by Maureen Myant

I was behind her in the post office queue when she fell. One second she was standing tall and proud, the next she was a crumpled heap on the floor. I put her in the recovery position, felt her pulse and called for an ambulance. No one else had a clue what to do. They stood around gawping until the woman behind the counter shooed them away.

'This isn't a sideshow, you know.' She called into the back for help while I tried to follow what the paramedics were saying on the phone. I did what they said but I was glad the ambulance didn't take too long.

'Are you a relative?' asked the paramedic.

I looked around to see what the post office assistant was doing. She was busy with customers, content to leave me to deal with the problem. I took a chance. 'I'm her great-niece.'

While we'd been waiting I'd looked in the old woman's bag to see if she had any means of identification. She was dressed expensively and I thought there might be something in it for me if I helped her. I had nothing better to do other than go home to my cold flat and search down the back of the sofa for pennies I knew weren't there. Maybe this way I'd get a cup of tea.

'What's her name, pet?

'Margaret McIntyre. Miss.' I said with confidence. 'Date of birth, 3rd January, 1942', and finished with her address. I knew the area where she lived. It was one of "The

Avenues", an estate agent's wet dream. A secluded street of large, sandstone houses only a mile or two from where I lived. Sometimes I walked round there at night trying to catch a glimpse of the impressive front rooms, dreaming about living there one day. As if. Perhaps I'd even seen this woman. I didn't think so though. I'd have recognised her bearing anywhere. She'd held herself impressively for a woman of her age.

'Margaret, my name is Jan. I'm a paramedic. Can you hear me?' Margaret groaned in response.

'You're in an ambulance. We're taking you to the Queen Elizabeth University Hospital. Just you relax. You're in safe hands. And your niece is here.'

Margaret tried to speak. It wasn't clear but Jan understood alright.

She looked at me, puzzled. 'What does she mean, no niece?'

I moistened my lips. 'She'll be worried about me missing work.' I changed the subject. 'You don't think she could have had a stroke, do you?'

'Oh, best wait for the doctor, but you should be prepared for the worst.' The ambulance stopped. We had arrived.

Once I gave Margaret's details to the receptionist, I went back to where Jan was waiting to hand over her patient. 'I don't suppose I could get a cup of tea, could I? I haven't had anything since breakfast.'

Jan smiled. 'There's a vending machine in the waiting area. It has all sorts. You've got time to get something. Though you'd better be quick, she's been prioritised.'

I thought of the pound coin I'd found this morning. It wouldn't be enough. And then I remembered the heft of Margaret's bag. 'No, it's fine. I'll stay with her.' It would give me a chance to go through her bag properly – if I managed to get hold of it again. Jan had taken it from me in the ambulance and laid it beside Margaret on the stretcher.

'Well, I'll be off now. Another call's come in. I hope it goes well with your great-aunt.' Jan left and I was alone with

Margaret. She looked half dead. Before I could do or say anything, a nurse bustled up.

'Are you with this lady?'

'Um, yes.'

She handed me Margaret's handbag. 'Can you take her belongings please?'

'Who, me?' I couldn't believe my luck.

'Yes,' her eyebrows were raised; two slugs feasting on a pudding face. 'You are her niece, aren't you?' That's what I was told.'

'Great-niece. Yes, of course I'll take them.' I tried not to snatch the bag from her.

I was there for another three hours. Five doctors saw her in all, before telling me with sombre faces that she'd had a stroke and would be in hospital for some time. I did my best to play the worried relative, before I escaped with my booty.

The thought of going back to my cold flat depressed me. There was a leak in the roof which the landlord was doing his best to ignore and I couldn't afford to put on the heating. I decided to check out Margaret's place.

*

The neighbourhood looked even better than I recalled. Red and blonde sandstone houses stood back from the road with neat lawns in front and in some cases an avenue of trees lined up like sentries. I thought of the street of shabby tenements where I lived. The only greenery there, was weeds splurging from cracks in the pavement and a buddleia that had taken root in a gutter. It was hard to believe both places were part of the same city. I jingled the house keys in my pocket as I walked up the driveway imagining the house was mine. The storm doors were closed. In most parts of the city this meant no one was at home but just to make sure, I rang the doorbell, looking around for signs of a burglar alarm. Nothing. Good. A tinny tune rang out, some classic shit. As expected, there was no answer so I tried the keys in the locks. There were four keys – the old dear wasn't taking any chances – and I was so engrossed I didn't hear the approaching footsteps. The tap on my shoulder sent the keys flying into the air.

'Can I help you?' the voice had the peculiar drawl of the Glasgow bourgeoisie, heard only in people of a certain age and class.

'I'm not sure.' Somehow I managed to keep cool. 'Are you a friend of Margaret?'

'I'm her neighbour. And you are…?'

'Her great-niece.'

'Really?' The voice raised several tones, indignant. 'She's never mentioned any relatives.'

I tucked away that piece of information. 'Yes, well, it's a long story.' I turned once more to the task of opening this fortress, taking my time until at last the door opened. 'Would you like to come in for a coffee?' My hands were trembling, whether from lack of food or an abundance of adrenalin I couldn't say.

'I think I'd better.' The woman's lips pursed.

I felt the woman's eyes on me as we went into the hall. I turned round to stare back. 'You'll have to show me the kitchen. I've never been here before.'

Cold blue eyes pierced mine. 'She's lived here for a long time.'

'As I said, it's a long story.' My voice was tight. 'She and my mother didn't get on.'

'And you've suddenly made up? A likely story.'

Christ, she was like a terrier on the scent of vermin. I drooped against the wall and rubbed my forehead. For once I wasn't acting. I had a headache coming on. 'She's had a massive stroke. The hospital contacted me as her next of kin. It's touch and go.' I allowed my voice to break a little.

'You poor thing. What a shock for you.'

I nodded, relieved that she seemed to believe me. But I had relaxed too soon because her eyes narrowed and she pounced again. 'How did they know to contact you?'

'She had a little card in her purse with next of kin on it. She can't speak you know. She may never speak again.' I squeezed a tear out. 'My mother, her sister's daughter, is dead now. Perhaps Margaret and I can make up. It must mean something… I mean, that she had me down as her next of kin.'

That tear washed away the last of her scepticism. Some people can't cry to order but all I have to do is think of something painful – a Brazilian wax for example – and out they come. She placed a hand on my shoulder. 'I'm sure it does.' She bustled around making tea. I sat down at the kitchen table, feeling the ambient warmth enfold me.

'Does my aunt have many friends?'

'Oh no, dear. She never has visitors. That's why when I saw you at the door, I had to come and make sure you weren't a burglar. You can't trust anyone these days.' She gave a little tinkly laugh.

I smiled. 'Margaret is very lucky to have a caring neighbour like you.' Her laugh trilled out again.

Two cups of tea later she left, having extracted a name (false) and telephone number (also false) from me. Time to make hay. Miss McIntyre was anything if not methodical. Bank statements were in a filing cabinet, along with information on her investments. She was worth quite a bit by the looks of things. Close by was a little book with all her passwords and user names. It had PASSWORDS emblazoned across the cover. I'd seen notebooks like this in Waterstones and wondered who'd be daft enough to buy them. Now I knew. I ordered a few necessities from her Amazon account, to be delivered the next day. No way would the old bag be home by then. It was cash I wanted though. I had her pin number, a small scrap of paper inside her purse. But that was slim pickings – three hundred a day – and cash machines had all sorts of cameras now. Transferring it to my own account was a non-starter for obvious reasons. It was too much to hope that she kept cash in the house but I looked anyway. Everywhere. Inside drawers, teapots, biscuit jars, the freezer. Even inside the toilet cisterns. There were three. Why did one woman need three toilets? In desperation I looked under the mattress in what had to be the main bedroom. It was bigger than my flat. It was a long shot but there it was, several small piles of crisp fifty pound notes.

There was over ten thousand pounds. I knelt on the floor beside the bed and tried not to cry. My worries were over. A pulse throbbed at my right temple, my heart jumping around at the prospect of so much money. I should have grabbed it and run. Instead I hesitated. Conscience? Aye right. No, I smelled richer pickings. I sat on the edge of the bed and thought. Margaret McIntyre clearly had no imagination. Money under the mattress was plain stupid, so she might just be the kind of person to hide the family silver under the floorboards. But which ones?

I walked round the edge of the bedroom testing for loose boards. They were firm, but there was a slight rucking of the carpet near the door. I tugged at it until it lifted revealing a key. This was more like it. But what did it open? I passed it from hand to hand as I thought about the layout of the house. In the kitchen I'd tried a door that didn't open. A cellar?

I ran downstairs to test this out. Sure enough the key fitted and the door opened to a narrow flight of stairs. I turned on the light and made my way down the concrete steps.

The cellar was cold and damp. And gloomy. The single light bulb did little to illuminate the space. It was bare except for a large trunk.

My first feeling on looking inside was disappointment. It was full of clothes. Old clothes, musty and stained with age.

Not the treasure chest of silver I'd hoped for. Nor the pile of jewellery my greedy mind had imagined. I poked at it in a desultory way hoping to hear the clank of precious metals but there was nothing. I pulled the clothes out, perhaps there would be something I could wear, a vintage dress perhaps. A change from my usual jeans and t-shirts. When I got to the bottom of the chest I noticed that one of the bundles was lumpy and I prodded it. Sure enough it was hard. My mouth was dry as I unfolded the cloth. I was hoping to see some silver, or a statuette perhaps. Something valuable.

I peeled back the last fold of material and stifled a scream. Silly me. I laughed at my foolishness. It was a baby doll. Very old by the looks of things, a bit creased. A rag doll. I looked more closely. It was… sort of… real. Christ! I thrust it back into the chest and stuffed my hand in my mouth to stop my screams. My first instinct had been right.

I shut the chest and ran up the stairs. I'd grab the money I'd found and never return. But just before I reached the top the cellar door slammed. The movement startled me and I fell backwards landing awkwardly. I lay at the bottom of the stairs, stunned, every part of me aching. It was some time before I could move. Upstairs, someone was moving around. I crawled up the steps, taking my time. I didn't want to fall again. At the top I tried the door. It was locked.

'Hello!' I shouted. 'Is anyone there?'

The footsteps moved towards me. 'You thought you were so smart, didn't you? Thought you could fool an old woman, two old women even. Did you not realise I'd try your phone number, look up your name on the internet? Both false. Well I've got you now. You can just stay there until the police arrive. I'm going back to my house now to…..'

There was a gasp, a thump and then nothing.

'Hello, are you ok? Hello, I can explain, really I can. Please don't phone the police…'

There was no reply.

*

I don't know what happened to her. Heart attack? Cerebral haemorrhage? I hope someone comes looking for her soon. I've been here over a day now. I've gone beyond thirsty and hungry and I'm so cold. I'd put on some of the clothes in the chest but I can't bear the thought of opening it again and seeing that dead baby. I've screamed and shouted but the house is quite a way back from the road. Someone was at the door an hour or so ago but although I yelled and thumped at the cellar door, they left. Probably the phone and laptop I'd ordered. It would be one of those crap delivery firms. They'll have tossed the parcels into the back garden and left. But someone else will come soon. I hope…

A Miracle in August by Ian Donaldson

It was *unusually* hot in Glasgow. Cars sagged on burning rubber tyres, slow-cooking drivers and passengers at twenty miles per hour. On the opposite side of the road from me, tenement flats built of aniseed sandstone shimmered dangerously, undecided whether to remain standing or not. And I, sweating irritably, a queue of one, waited on a long overdue bus to ride into town.

A small fluttering caught my attention.

A butterfly.

I shivered suddenly as it tumbled over my head and then back into the road, just out of reach. The feeling lasted no more than a second – maybe less? And in that fraction of time, *I* was that small body, straining, pushing, *willing* myself forward – determined to overcome the single overwhelming problem of the moment.

The fragile Kamikaze changed direction again, tossed one way, and then another, on the hot, unpredictable breeze; displaying impossible angles of flight, determined to cross the road it seemed, regardless of the colossal odds against it on completing its hazardous journey.

SMASH!

The huge red truck thundered dumbly on, unaware of the violence and destruction it had wreaked in the universe.

'NO!' I screamed inside. *'Please, no …'*

The butterfly lay motionless, wings folded, a pale, ivory triangle against the dull gray surface of the road.

The wind held its breath.

I held my breath too.

A bus appeared from the same direction as the hit-and-run lorry. It diesel-roared past, hauling the innocent aviator up in its wake, causing it to cartwheel and smash silently to the ground for a second time.

Once again, as delicate as moon gold china, the butterfly, lay perfectly still, immersed in summer noon brightness.

Sadness hit me like a slow-moving tidal wave. I didn't know what to do or who to call or how long it was before I blinked. If it wasn't already dead, the butterfly must surely be in pain. It was then that my heart made a decision.

I felt the bag I'd been clutching at my side slip from my fingers, and without looking to left or right, I stepped off the pavement to put an end to this beautiful creature's agony.

The world around me stopped, car engines faded to nothing, and my footsteps ceased to make any sound. As I got closer, I thought I saw the butterfly's miniature yacht sail wings twitch. *Maybe* it was still alive? *No.* Surely, it could have only been the breeze, pushing mindlessly at the tiny road victim. When I reached the crime scene, I raised my right foot to bring peace – to be *God*.

The butterfly's wings stirred again, and then seemed to quiver, only this time – with *life*. They quivered *again* – as though nature's elemental engine had fired up before the spark of life, the butterfly still possessed was extinguished and lost. My foot hung in the air as the tiny wonder began to rise, uncertain at first, like a drunken pilot. Higher and higher it climbed into the suddenly, still air, growing in confidence, responding to the irresistible pull of life, leaving death, empty-handed and far below.

As soft as a whisper, my foot touched the surface of the earth again. Hands shielding my watering eyes, I watched the butterfly's miraculous ascent, until its tiny wings disappeared from view into the blinding sun's embrace.

No Shelter From The Storm by Tracey McBain

"Wee, sleekit, cowrin, tim'rous beastie, O, what a panic's in thy breastie!"

Jimmy is reciting his favourite poem in hushed tones while, from the tram window, watching men on ladders extinguish lights in glass lanterns. As the gentle flames dim one by one, their glow is replaced by the soft pink of dawn.

Others may reel off a prayer but Jimmy, not a man for religion, prefers the words of the Bard to those of the Lord. He'll take his comfort where he bloody well pleases, thank you very much. He looks up to pluck the next line of the poem from the air but instead sees the tram conductor move toward him.

"Bloody hell," Jimmy thinks, locking eyes with the man. The conductor, spotting his prey, scurries over and loudly asks, "What do you make of the news, then?" Jimmy opens his mouth to reply but the conductor, rattling loose change in his pocket pushes on, "I was jist sayin' to the missus last night this is where it wis headin. But what will happen noo? Ma boy..."

A loud 'clang' signals his stop. Jimmy smiles weakly as he rises, swiftly moving to the back of the tram and shaking off the night shift like dandruff from his cropped salt and pepper hair. He isn't unsympathetic; after all, he has his own precious boy to think of, currently tucked up in bed warm and snug. As if to remind him of that the soft morning air caresses his face as he steps onto the pavement. He pauses briefly to watch the tram, its back end shuggling like a child riding a bicycle at breakneck speed.

Jimmy gazes across at an island in the middle of the wide road, the site of a newly built tram shelter, elegant despite its modest size. The sparkling cream and green tiles smother the building like frosting on a cake. But this is no confection. The shelter with its own clock tower and turrets stands confident, defiant almost, demanding to be admired. He thinks the shelter has been built in a fancy style called 'art nouveau.' Jimmy had read about it in The Herald. If it was printed there then it must be true, mustn't it? As a typesetter for the newspaper facts imprint on his brain the way the typeface marks paper.

He crosses the road briskly, the sun now rising as quickly as warm dough and heads into the shelter waiting area. His shadow elongates his gangly frame until he looks like a caricature staring out from a fun house mirror. His pale face and hazel eyes in small-rimmed glasses peer back from the glass of the tram shelter door, still smelling faintly of paint.

"Morning Sandy," he says in a low voice to the man sitting on dark wooden benches, flat cap obscuring his face. The cap is ancient but has gripped the memory of Sandy's carrot coloured hair, now the shade - and texture - of wheat. Sandy lifts his head and grins as he sees his friend walk toward him.

"Whit's happenin' in the world?" asks Sandy, while packing tobacco into a small pipe.

This is the normal morning routine for Jimmy and Sandy. Like cogs in the printing machinery at the newspaper. One in and one out. One out and one in.

Jimmy whips out his rolled-up newspaper from the pocket of his shabby tweed jacket. He flicks it open in front of Sandy who, like a child excited to read 'The Broons' on a Sunday morning, aligns on an advertisement in the bottom corner.

"Pettigrew's sale!" Sandy exclaims, rubbing his hands together. "Now we're talkin'! Ah need a pair o' new boots. Look at the state of these," he says, showing Jimmy the worn out sole. "Your Edward's there, eh? Think he could sort me oot?"

It gives Jimmy a lift to hear Sandy mention Edward and his job at Pettigrews, a very grand department store, which The Herald had once described as "Glasgow's Harrods." An office job there no less. He's going places that boy. It was all there for the taking. He could be his own boss one day. Fancy that. His lad, his boy, giving the orders not taking them.

Jimmy sighs loudly. Like an exasperated teacher pointing at a blackboard he taps on the headline,

GREAT BRITAIN DECLARES WAR ON GERMANY!

"Ach well, it's bin on the cards since that Archduke bloke wis murdered" Sandy says with a shrug. "it'll no matter tae us anyways, we're too old. Five score year and ten and aw that."

Jimmy rolls his eyes, "It's three score year and ten ya wee eejit. And that would mean we're seventy! Three twenties and a ten. Seventy!"

"I thought that meant forty." Sandy replies slyly. "Ah never did listen in Sunday School."

It was impossible to be angry with Sandy. As a ten year old, he had contracted polio that had left him with a withered leg and withered attitude to life which perplexed and amused his old friend in equal measure. Sandy was like a non-swimmer throwing himself off a pier with the intention of learning on the way down. Always living in the moment.

"You should have seen the boys at work," Jimmy says, "running around like they'd been given another fair fortnight off work. A few of them were talkin' about enlistin'."

"Aye ye can see how the yung 'uns want a bit of a lark. Anyhoo. Look at the state of us, they'd pay us a pretty penny no to sign up!" Sandy replies while pointing first to his leg and then to Jimmy's glasses.

Jimmy smiles and shakes his head before soberly saying, "I don't mind tellin' you, I feel lucky that my Edward is too young. Just turned 17. Not long aff being a bairn." He wants to talk more about Edward. He wants to say how much he loves him, how much he reminds him of his wife, long dead, that without him he would, like a sunflower with no sun, fold in on himself and fade away. The feelings flow like the River Cart bursting its banks, but the words tangle up inside him like stubborn weeds beneath the water, choking amy chance of breaking free.

Instead, he finishes lamely, "Ye know?"

Sandy nods as he stands up. He does know. That's the thing with best friends, they are like deep sea divers, finding treasure on the ocean bed while the rest of the world remains oblivious above. "There's ma tram, half past 6 on the dot. And Jimmy," he pauses, touching his friends' arm, "Don't fret. This thing will be over afore we know it. Six months tops mark ma words. Edward will be fine. You worry too much aboot him. I'll see you the morra. Remember the boots!"

Jimmy shakes his head, folds the newspaper, and places it back in his pocket. As he turns, he looks across the road to the Victoria Infirmary hospital standing proud and upright like its namesake, bathed in the soft light of a new day. It was a marvel. And full of mod cons. Electricity for one. It even had a machine that could take a picture of the inside of you. Imagine that! Actually see your bones. Whatever would they think of next.

Turning left, Jimmy strides toward Battlefield Road, signs of morning in full bloom. A delivery boy is peddling his bike, basket full of bread and eggs. Behind, a small black dog chases him, barking. Men slowly make their way to work, heads bent in the low sun, preoccupied with their own thoughts. The air feels heavy and still - like a Hogmanay hangover but without the party.

Everything has changed and yet nothing has changed. Yesterday men went to work as they are doing today, but the world is spinning on a tilted axis, hurtling toward a new trajectory. Every single nerve ending in Jimmy's body feels agitated and raw the more he thinks about how life could change for Edward. He takes a deep breath to calm his clamoring heart. "It'll be all over soon and he won't need to be involved," he thinks. "Sandy's right fir once, six months tops, seven at a push. But definitely under a year."

As he approaches his soot clad tenement building, perched on top of a grocers, he notices net curtains flutter in the first-floor window. It's Mrs Gilfedder, his elderly neighbour, "now she is three score years and ten," he thinks wryly. With those powers of observation and her Aberdonian lilt she would make a fine spy. Guard the perimeter Mrs Gilfedder!

Jimmy is nearly bowled over by someone exiting the close at speed. It's Edward, the human cannonball. Tall and narrow, he has freckled skin, blond hair and large blue eyes. His teeth protrude slightly; Sandy had once said the lad could eat an apple through a tennis racket. Cheeky bugger!

"Edward, you're runnin' like you've stolen sumthin," Jimmy shouts. "Who says I huvnae?" Edwards replies, grinning confidently.

"Haven't! Not huvnae!" his father instinctively corrects, before asking "Why the hurry, laddie?"

Edward glances at the newspaper in his father's pocket. He starts to ask, "is there any news? The boys at work were saying..."

"Oh this," Jimmy nods his head toward his pocket, "yesterday's paper, ah picked it up by mistake. Ye know whit it's like at the printin' press, mad at times."

Edward knits his brows but doesn't ask to see it. He knows better than to push it with his father. Over the years, ever since his mother died when he was eight, he has got used to managing his dad's many moods and gestures. He knows his father worries about him, always asking where he's going, who he's with, what he wants for dinner, but honestly at seventeen it's time for that to stop.

Playing along with the charade, because why not, Edward carries on, neatly pulling his shirt cuffs out of his jacket, " I told you, the summer sale starts today, we all need to be in early, office staff too. Doors open at nine and Hector says it's going to be mobbed."

Jimmy thinks he's got away with it. Edward clearly doesn't know yet. Good, that's very good. For this brief moment he can cling to the last shreds of a world that isn't tainted and scorched.

"Hector?" Jimmy queries, trying to keep the conversation going.

"From Pettigrews! I've told you about him before - we work together, he's the one I take my lunch with," Edwards replies, frowning fleetingly, a familiar exasperation in his eyes.

Jimmy remembers now - he suddenly feels very tired.

"Home at the usual time? It's your favourite tonight - mince and tatties," Jimmy says steering the subject to safer ground.

"I'm going to the new Picture House in Shawlands tonight, I told you yesterday," Edward replies.

"Who's the lucky lassie?" Jimmy teases.

Edward gives a soft smile. "No lassie Dad. Just me and Hector. He lives in Pollokshields, so we'll meet in the middle. We're going to see the new Charlie Chaplin picture. Look there's my tram, I need to run, or I'll be late."

"Of course, son, I'm glad you've got a friend. Like me and Sandy, eh?" he replies.

Edward doesn't reply, he wants to leave before he hears it. He runs toward the shelter, effortlessly weaving through dazed pedestrians. I'm proud of you son.

Jimmy stands looking after his boy, 'I'm proud of you son!" he shouts at his back.

As he turns to enter the close, he remembers. "The boots! Those bloody boots," he says with a loud sigh. "That Sandy will be the death of me."

******

Like a game of pass the parcel, summer turns to autumn and then to winter, each new season a fresh layer of horrors. Every headline is now home to someone's shattered reality. In sympathy, the weather cries the tears of mothers as news of the casualties come in. The Herald has devoted a special section to the fallen. Men from all over the country reduced to grey, grainy faces, their lives written as if on the back of a fag packet.

"Did ye see the McPherson lad's been killed?" Sandy asks, his voice unusually low and hoarse as he and Jimmy sit in the tram shelter in late December. The windows are covered in condensation, offering little warmth against the cold, damp day. People go about their business, but they seem weighed down, as if they have stones in their pockets. A young boy sits next to his mother on the edge of the bench, his legs swinging restlessly. Everyone in the shelter watches him, searching for the faces of their own boys, now grown and in foreign lands.

"Aye and big Davy Cameron, the milkman from Young's Dairy," Jimmy replies while reading the headline: "The Great War: New Battle Strategies."

Sandy glances over and says "Ha! Fancy bloody headline that. "The 'Great War," my arse," he mutters. "Mair like the "Great Disappearance." There's hardly any yung yins left." After a short pause he then asks while looking at Jimmy's stony profile, "And eh, speaking of yung yins, er, how's your Edward?"

Sandy knows fine well how Edward is. He got the story when Edward dropped off his new boots. Leaning against an old oak dresser in the kitchen, Sandy had listened while puffing on his old pipe.

"The day war was declared he didn't want to tell me. The newspaper was in his pocket all along. I pretended not to notice. Told him I was going to work because of the sale." Edward had said irritation prickling across his skin. "Since then, I've been begging to go. Most of the lads from work are away. How stupid will I look when they all come back?"

"Yer da is just lookin' out for ye, laddie." Sandy replies, taking a deep drag on his pipe, the smoke settling around him like a shroud.

"I know he is, but he treats me like a child, and I've gone along with it to keep the peace, but I can't. I'm not eight anymore," Edward finishes, wiping a little spittle away with the back of his hand.

"Ye think marchin' aff tae war is gonna make him see ye any different? You think he'll wave ye aff happy as larry?"

"I'm not asking for permission; I'm asking for help. Make him see sense," Edward replied, his eyes a mix of anger and desperation.

Sandy had sighed, the weight of Edward's words pressing on him like the printing press he operated every day.

"You're askin' me for sense?" Sandy said trying to lighten the mood. "A pipe smokin' midget wae scarecrow hair?"

Edward managed a reluctant smile, "A funny, pipe smokin' midget wae scarecrow hair." And after a pause, "And who knows my dad better than anyone."

In the shelter Jimmy repeats Sandy's question. "How's Edward? Aye fine thanks. Working away. Always busy. Anyway - did you finally put a line on that horse you fancied at Hamilton? You've been talkin' about it long enough."

"Aye, sometimes ye need to admit defeat, let go and take a chance, don't ye think?" Sandy replies slowly, locking his gaze with Jimmy. There is a heavy silence, filled with unspoken dread; a quiet acknowledgement of a deeper understanding between them.

"I do know, aye I do," Jimmy replies quietly. Sandy ignores the tear running down Jimmys cheek because sometimes that's what friends need to do.

******

In town that afternoon Mrs Gilfedder is treating herself to a new hat. "No one else is going to buy one for me," she thinks sourly. Loneliness can be a curse.

She takes the tram from Battlefield all the way to the top of Hope Street and will walk the short distance to Pettigrews on Sauchiehall Street. It's a cold day, a wild wind whipping around her ankles like it might lash them together.

Despite the weather, the streets are busy. She prefers this part of town. The lady shoppers are elegant in their wide brimmed hats and corseted coats. The children are clean and neat and tidy – just the way she likes them. There are a few men – mostly older men of course now. Mrs Gilfedder is looking forward to the admiring glances she knows she will get when she takes her hat box back on the tram home. She might even treat herself to an afternoon tea at Miss Cranston's Willow Tea Rooms.

In the distance she can hear voices echoing around the wide street. Ladies' voices at that. Ladies shouldn't raise their voices. "Cowards! Why don't you take the kings shilling?" one of them shouts. Was it those Suffragettes at it again? Always on about something that lot.

Mrs Gilfedder hurries toward the fracas which appears to be coming from The Pettigrews building itself. Looming majestically against the grey skyline, it is the very height of Victorian grandeur, with palatial facades adorned with intricate stone carvings and grand archways.

She now has the measure of the situation. Five well-dressed young ladies have formed a circle and break ranks rushing toward any man who passes looking like he might be fit for service. "What would their parents think?" Mrs Gilfedder muses to herself. The ladies are forcibly handing over white feathers. Some men try to steer around the group, but they are relentlessly hunted down. She sees one man who has a limp, stand still in shock as the Suffragette places the feather into his waistcoat while shouting in his face "You coward! Why haven't you enlisted?"

Mrs Gilfedder tuts and moves around the corner toward the entrance of the store; she can see the doorman ready to swing open the large glass door for her to sweep in. Out of the corner of her eye she spots two young men exiting from the opposite side. She has a perfect view of one of them – one has dark slicked back hair, dark eyes and wide grin. The other has blond hair.

What to do? It's cold outside and she wants to get her hat. But she could easily warn them, tell them to turn left not right, save themselves for another day. But don't the young ones want to sign up? That's what the papers are saying. And who is she to interfere anyway? She's not a lady who shouts in the street.

She watches casually as the boys turn the corner straight into the mob. She can hear them coming at them, it sounds like the whole troop are baying for them like one of those Wild West pictures showing in the new Shawlands Picture House.

It's only then that she spots him. "Oh, would you look at that. It's young Edward," she says to herself while sniffing up into one nostril. "Miss Cranston can keep her fancy teas; I'll get away home and let the faither ken."

Edward purposefully climbs the stairs of the close that evening, a few shillings rattling his pocket. As he approaches his front door, the gas light on the landing ahead of him flickers and dances transforming his normally upright figure into a shadowy specter against the wall.

He knows there will be a scene and he's ready for it. Has been ready for months. He knows exactly what to say. It's his life and he's going to do things his way. Anyway, it's too late. He's gone and enlisted. So there. He cringes slightly. It sounds like he is about to tell his father 'nana nana na,' like a spoilt child.

Pulling his shoulders back he opens the front door and heads into the kitchen. Jimmy is sitting at the old pine table still with his hands clasped in front of him.

"Son, I've been waitin' for ye," he says. Edward can see his father has been crying. "Sit doon."

Edward does as he is told although his heart feels like it has vaulted into his throat, pounding so fiercely he can barely catch his breath.

"Ah know," Jimmy says voice cracking.

"H-how?" Edward stammers.

Jimmy points his index finger down indicating Mrs Gilfedder's flat below. "Couldn't wait to tell me, said she tried to warn you to stay away from the crowd." They both raise their eyebrows in mutual scoff.

"As if," Edward mutters.

Jimmy tries to soften the mood saying, "If Sandy was here, he'd ask where the feathers come from anyway?" In his best Sandy voice, he says," It's no like Glesga's hoachin' wae wee white doves."

Jimmy's smile fades, replaced by an etched sorrow, "I'm sorry that happened tae ye son. I take it you've gone and signed up"

"Black Watch," Edward replies simply.

"Be careful son, please come home tae me. Here. Take this," Jimmy says while removing his wedding ring. His fingers are so skinny it comes off easily.

"I can't – you love that ring, it's the last thing you have of mums."

Jimmy reaches and places it in Edward's palm, closing it over with his own hand; they sit in silence, hands clasped together while the raindrops lash down, silently mocking them from the window.

******

Two weeks later, on a dull, dry winter's morning, Jimmy walks Edward to the tram shelter. Not long ago he was a bairn playing toy soldiers and here he is one himself. On the pavement he embraces Edward, feeling his bony shoulders through the coarse fabric of his uniform, holding him as if he were still that small grieving boy from years ago.

Edward breaks free first. "I'll write," he says softly. Every week. I promise." He starts to run to the tram, turns and smiles that sweet buck toothed grin of his. As Edward jumps on the back of the tram Jimmy notices the same conductor who was worried about his own boy all those months ago. They are now tethered in a way neither of them ever wanted. The conductor gives him a gentle salute.

Jimmy watches as the tram takes off down the road, the metallic screech of wheels echoing against the quiet morning. As Edward disappears, he knows that part of their souls will, for an eternity, be rooted to this spot.

He turns and walks toward the shelter where he knows Sandy is waiting for him.

The Linden Blossom by Slava Konoval

The linden blossom
soaked in moisture
touches the swirling petals
which drown in island puddles.

Impressed by the golden camouflage,
inflorescence of green perfume
quietly sleeps in the leaves.

The grass grows under the cherry tree,
it laughs at the neighbour's jokes,
the people missed the green silence.

Lonely columns of herb are falling,
from walking cat of colour sturgeon,
swaying rocking dandelion and thyme boats,
sweat drips from the moustachioed forehead.

A wild hunter hides,
behind a thick iron wall,
the sloth liked the shade of the columns.

Inside The Circle by Frank Chambers

'Hello.'

'Hi Craig. It's Gordie. Just called to say there's a meet up in the Church tonight. Thought you might want to come along.'

'A meet up? What do you mean?'

'Just some of the boys getting together for a drink.'

'From inside the Cir....' I stopped himself from saying the word and feigned a cough to cover my faux pas. 'Sorry, got a bit of a cold, Gordie.'

'The boys are all brand new Craig. You'll like them. The reason I think you should come is there may be someone coming who can get you a start in the bank.'

'Really!'

'He's good mates with someone in H.R.'

'Aye okay, I'll come. What time?'

'Eight.'

'See you there.'

'Great.'

'That was Gordie, dad. I'm going to meet him for a pint.'

'Wise up son. Your pal's inside the Circle now and you're outside. You'll be seeing less and less of him. Better get used to it.'

'Will you stop calling it that? I nearly said it myself on the phone. Good job Gordie was on the train and he didn't notice.'

'I think The Circle is the perfect name, describes exactly what it is.'

'Will you give it a rest? We are literally the only family in Glasgow that calls it that. When Gordie is in here, you better not say a word about, "The Circle". He'll think we're all bloody nuts.'

'Me, say anything! I don't think there is much danger of that. You'll be lucky if Gordie ever deigns to darken our door again. And another thing, it will be Gordon not Gordie from now on. You mark my words. It'll be like your Uncle Tommy all over again. Weddings and funerals, that's the only time we ever see him.'

'He was here last month dad.'

'Well there must have been a blue moon in the sky'.

'It was a Saturday afternoon as you know very well.'

'Aye, well he was hardly here five minutes, hardly worth mentioning. Don't know why he bothered taking his coat off. I've spent more time on the pan.'

'I'll not argue with that, but Tom was here for over an hour.'

'Tom! It was Tommy till his elevation into the Circle. I suppose we are lucky it's not Thomas.'

'Give it a rest dad,will you. I'll need to go.'

When my da's about to go off on one of his rants its best just to get out of the house. There's nothing I've not heard a hundred times before: downfall of the working man, betrayal of their own community, social climbers, they only have time for each other. I could add another dozen cliches to the list.

So that was me out on the street, with two hours to kill, before meeting my mate.

There is something that I have never let on about to dad. I tried to get inside "The Circle" myself. I didn't get through the vetting process. Application rejected. No reasons given. Personally, I think it was because I didn't earn enough. Hence the search for a new job. All the palaver I went through and it wasn't even guaranteed to be permanent. I could have been tossed out in six months.

I did tell my mum what I was doing. She thought it was a great idea. 'You'll mix with a better class of people Craig, you go for it,' she said. I think that was a wee dig at my dad. I was only thinking I would have somewhere better to go for a drink.

It was all very different for Gordie. Straight in, permanent member right from the off. No references, no vetting and no probation for him. Both his parents were all for it. In fact, I think it was more their idea than Gordie's. His dad smoothed the way, knew all the right people to talk to. Gordie's good job in the bank helped of course.

Well anyway, how was I going to fill those two hours? First I waited for the bus down to Main Street when it would have been quicker to walk. My next move was to go for a coffee and a baguette, even though coffee shops aren't really my thing.

The only one the town had to offer was shut. That left the pubs.

I discarded The Bull straight away. Billy and John would be in there. Billy would have shoved a pint into my hand, ignoring that I was only wanting a soft drink. John would get me a second pint before I was half way through the first, then Billy would be telling me it's my round before I had started on that second pint. No, on second thoughts, he would just order three pints at the bar then tell me to get my hand in my pocket. Then I'd be trying to down two pints before they downed one. That would be no mean feat, but my only chance of escaping, before Billy gets another round in and the whole process starts all over again. No, the Bull was definitely out.

That gave me another half dozen pubs to consider, but I was bound to know someone, no matter which one I chose. That would also mean getting stuck in the old round system. They would buy me a drink then I would buy them one back. Of course I'd need to get one for myself as well to keep them company, pub etiquette. I did not want to meet Gordie and his new "Circle" mates, half pissed so that ruled out passing the time in any of the local pubs.

Apart from the drink, there was also the danger of someone asking me where I was headed. Not an easy question to answer, depending on the company. Take John and Billy for instance.

They're best mates but there are two topics it is always best to avoid when you're with them. One is football, John being a Celtic supporter and Billy a Rangers man. They could talk away on the subject to each other okay, but add a third party and it could turn into World War Three. The other topic to avoid was, "The Circle." Not that they would ever call it that.

Still an hour and a half to go and my options were limited. The 90 bus would take me straight there and drop me right outside the Church, but it would get me there an hour early. I decided to take the train into the city centre, then another train back out to the Southside.

I arrived just after eight. Gordie was standing at the bar in a group of five guys. Everyone had a bottle in their hand. No two bottles were the same brand. Gordie said. 'What are you for?'

I could see them all looking askance when I said. 'Just get me a pint of heavy.' I had revealed myself straight away as being from outside the Circle.

I recognised one of the guys in the group, played against him in the amateur league. He was a dirty bastard, took the legs right away from me when I was clear through on goal. It was clearly inside the box, a stone wall penalty kick. The referee just waved play on. Gary Williamson was his name.

I never let on when Gordie did the introductions. I don't know if he recognised me, but he gave me a right strong handshake, slapped me on the back and said. 'Good to meet you Craigy'. I thought, hope he's not the guy from the bank.

To use rhyming slang, I thought they were all bankers. Every one of them was new to the Circle and each one was absolutely full of it. I sat there for the first hour nodding my head, as one after the other extolled on how life was so much better now that they were in the Circle. I felt a tad out of things. To be fair, they did try to include me in the conversation but no matter where a discussion started, it always ended up back at the Circle.

When my own failed attempt at getting in came up, there was no end of advice. When I said I thought it was simply because I didn't earn enough, there was synchronised nodding of heads followed by a long embarrassing silence.

Gordie broke the hush by asking if I wanted to meet up the next day to watch the rugby.

'The rugby?' I asked, astonished that Gordie was watching rugby.

'We're all going.' The others nodded their agreement and gave encouragement for me to say yes.

'In here?'

'No in a pub up at the cross.'

'But will they not be showing the football, it's the cup final.'

'Only in the small bar, the rugby will be on the big screen.'

'Sure, I'll come along.'

Well, what a surprise that was. Gordie Stuart watching the rugby when there was football on at the same time. It was okay for me, my team didn't reach the final, but his had. I zoned out of the conversation for a minute or two while I took that in. Wait till my dad hears that one, I thought, then decided it was best never to mention it.

When the actual banker revealed himself it was Alasdair, the one with the weakest handshake. He was actually very nice. The first thing he told me was that he couldn't pull any strings, but he would give me as much information as he could about what qualities the bank was looking for. By the time we finished talking it was last orders.

All in all, it had been a great night. The boys turned out to be, as Gordie put it, 'brand new'. There was no pressure to drink too much and the conversation was more interesting than in my usual Friday night haunt. Alasdair had given me some useful advice. If it didn't get me a job in his bank, I could use it somewhere else. I was happy and relaxed. Too relaxed.

The words just came out and no amount of coughing could cover it up.

'The Circle really is the place to be. I'm going to try again to get in.'

Five blank faces stared at me. It took a second before I realised what I'd said. The heat started rising up my neck.

'The Circle?' I don't know what blank face said it but they were all awaiting an explanation. Seeing as it was my dad that came up with stupid name I had no hesitation in laying the blame on him.

'It's just something my dad says. It's his name for this place.'

The faces were still every bit as blank.

'It's a compliment actually. Shows he thinks it's special, a pretty cool place.' Not at all what my dad thinks but what could I say.

'You mean this pub?' Gordie asked.

'No, the whole area. He calls it, "inside the circle".'

'I don't get it.' It was clear the others didn't either.

'The Circle, the Cathcart Circle. You all live inside the Cathcart Circle.'

'Right.' Four faces returned to more or less normal, one looked more puzzled than ever. It was the Paisley footballer.

Gordie explained. 'You know the train you get out of Central.' Gary nodded. 'It goes Pollokshields West, Maxwell Park.' Again Gary nodded. 'Well some of the trains go round the southside in a loop, ending up at Queens Park and Pollokshields East then back to Central. Cathcart is the station at the middle of that loop, so its called the Cathcart Circle.'

'I see.' Gary's tone suggested he did nothing of the kind.

'It's just that all the best bits of the Southside are inside that circle.' I added

'Your dad's a genius, Craig.' Alisdair said. ' It's true. All the good pubs, the best restaurants, the interesting shops. They are all inside the circle.'

'All the nicest flats too.' I chipped in.

As we downed our last drink, exceptions to the rule were searched for but few were found.

'You have got to bring your dad tomorrow.' Gordie demanded. 'He's going to be a legend around here.'

'He has arranged to go down to the bowling club once the football is finished.' I omitted to say, 'only if the right team wins.'

Good nights were exchanged under the magnificent columned doorway of the converted Church, before I slipped into my Uber.

Down the hill, along Battlefield Road and under the railway bridge and I was out of the Circle. Before me, the long stretch of suburbia, then home. I turned my head and whispered under my breath. 'I'll be back.'

Marian's ghosts fae Langside by Ian Goudie

Ane hunner 'n' fifty lang deid souls
languish beneath the Queens Park scum
ancient battle cries o' ghosts 'n' ghouls
unheard fir hauf a millennium
'We huv ance mair a Queen,' thair boast

Thou ance thay wur sax thoosan strang
muckle mair than the Regent's force
o' hagbutters wi' boar spears sae lang
huily mairching ahin Moray's horse
bit Argyll's infantry still loast

Herries' calvary haed turnt back
forces on fit focht pouss 'n' pike
pints stickit in opponents' jacks
'til Mary's dowe airmy teuk flicht
lea'in fawen billies as ghosts

In little mair time than an oor
13th May 1568
she loast hairt like ne'er afore
fir the last time takin the gate
Mary Stuart last Queen o' Scots

Ian Goudie
The Killie Poet

Ruder Forms Survive by Jonathan Charles Napier

The upland riverbank along the White Cart Water climbed sheer to a stone wall that was capped with concrete and crowned with an iron stretcher railing and ran the whole length of the river. The morning sky was clear and taut as a drumskin, and the bare sunlight skewed the railing in dark bars on the walking path and the ladder of its shadow drew over them steadily, as they walked side by side in injured silence.

His fawny beard and hair were unshorn and the linen shirt he wore looked heavy on his sunken shoulders. Sunny passersby who looked to exchange casual pleasantries received no such acknowledgements in return. Played out on his countenance were the chaotic, unseeable machinations of his mind; his jaw trembled like a stopped flue and the jut of his brow was pulled grotesquely low over eyes, red raw.

She likewise struggled to hide that she was mostly shell and little spirit that morning. Her expression was unnaturally straight, as though her surface clung desperately to an imitation of herself. Her bony cheeks glowed with rash from repeated wiping, and her lips were chapped and scarlet against her pallor. She wore a blousy red shirt over all white vest, shorts, and shoes, and a silver anklet that chimed high over the stifling atmosphere. The humidity so smothered the air that every sound reverberated doubly, and her dirge impressed that she towed some unseen burden.

She sought her hand's perch in the crook of his arm, but he resisted with the subtle cowering of some lame creature that wished its insignificance to remain unimpeded, even if by compassion. She was persistent however, and in the second instance, though he feebly shrunk from her again, she gripped his arm and reared him with ease.

The ladder of shadow paused over them, and the anklet chime ceased. Her eyes were raw like his but still bright and deep; she held up to him her face bare of guile or tactic, but he would not look out from under his brow.

'I know you're suffering right now,' she said, with her eyes attended fully to his burned-out features, 'but you're not on this walk by yourself, so, could we please…'

The gurgle of the river echoed on in the warm stillness. Somewhere a magpie called and waited and called again and behind that solemn rattle, as though for its own amusement, a goldfinch sang.

At length he met her gaze and somewhere in this shared attention he conceded to her plea and offered her the crook of his arm, and they proceeded interlinked and chiming with every other step.

So blinding was the sun and so azure its vault that morning, that all the buildings and structures of the earth were darkened in its light; shadowed tenement roofs and chimney tops chipped out the skyline in dark shards and were illuminated only by sunbeams caught in windowpanes, that shone like absurd stars.

The stifling heat, the blinding sunlight, and walking too long in silence found expression in her short choice of words.

'You did get some good news too you know,' she said, and the chiming stopped.

He shot a hard look at her, and she spun from his glare as though it struck her. She spurned the bloodshot eyes that mapped wildly her face, as though searching her for some spurious cause or desire for rebuke but, finding neither, merely detached from her. She did not resist as he slid his arm from her grasp and restationed himself before the stone wall. Robin song unwound from within the blackberry bushes that fruited over the wall and through the iron rungs.

Where they were stopped, a gap in the high river forest offered a clear view of the White Cart Water as it ran towards them. So narrowed the river through Battlefield that its corridor was almost bridged by boughs of cypress and hawthorn, the roots of which were rooted long and deep into the bluff side. At the bank side, a jungle of purple willowherb grew tall over long grass, and giant hogweed sprouted in columnar stalks, its florets like lace umbrellas that almost grazed the overarching trees.

He peered over the railing at a crop of herculean hogweed stalks severed and their fine umbels stove in, and he saw where the tall grass eroded at the riverbank; those edge-most culm, whose inflorescence so burdened the integrity of their blades that they arched like keyholes and seemed to thirst for the passing water. He saw the water, and the water was empty.

'Not a single duck to be seen,' he said. The words rasped out of him like they hurt to speak, and he cleared his throat with a noise like the cranking of a dry engine. The robins in the bushes hushed their little romances.

'They'll be there.' Though cracked too, her voice held its assuredness, and her assumption spoke to a familiarity they shared with the river life.

She joined his side at the railing and looked through the gap in the weeds and into the sunlit water. The silty channel riffled contentedly over grey stone beaches and the water sprayed off the rocks and rose over the river and its mist smelled of ammonia and faintly of sewage. She looked upriver and then downriver, and down the grassy bank and along the white tide weaving amongst the stones, and she too saw that there were no ducks in the river.

'Of all days.'

'They'll be there somewhere,' she said, her voice still mustering a brightness. The river went on flushing past them and their chiming resumed in time.

When they reached the park, they crossed the road and entered into a stream of riotous noise from the ante-courts that housed a playpark on one side and pitches fenced-in by steel poles on the other. A collective and constant squealing emanated from the swarm of children who spun on colourful wood, slid on polished steel, and climbed on a giant rope pyramid; the parents harked after the children, barking names and instructions, only to be rebuted with yet more screaming. The noise rolled out, uninterrupted, and was accompanied by the irregular gong that tolled their walk in uncertain cycles, as a lone boy battered his football off the fence poles.

They waded through the noise between neat rows of slender linden trees that lined the central avenue to where it split like a hayfork, its left and right tines both shaded by the mingling canopies of a glade of linden trees with crowns like titanic mushroom caps. They took the left fork and were delivered into a chamber of foliage; an Edenic glade, its carpet white clover and its walls a lush hedgerow, wherein the noise of the children was deadened. Her chime could be heard again, was enchanting in the solemnity, and was then halted in the middle of the path.

'That doctor who called, was he the one that we met with before?'

'I think he was the one you met the first or second time.'

'That one who used the term "unwarranted" in my appointment?' A profound resentment filled his voice but blinked itself out again like candleflame on a blackened wick. 'At least he was nicer on the phone this morning.' Doves cooed over them.

'I always said that I didn't want them enough anyway. I suppose I felt that was true, at least at the time.'

'I always said that I didn't want them at all. Famous last words.'

'That's something everyone says at some point. I've said it myself.'

'I'm ashamed to admit it,' he looked into her eyes as he spoke, 'but a part of me had hoped that the blame lay with you.'

Though she might have accepted and appreciated his candour in some shared echelon of humanity, and the corners of her smile fought earnestly to present as much, her eyes could not help but betray the wounding from his words, and any false levity was stripped from her expression.

'I'm not telling you that to hurt you, but I need to be honest that I had such a vicious hope, because maybe that's the sort of thinking the world needs less of. Maybe that's why I'm being punished, because I think in such horrible ways.'

'This isn't some punishment you've earned.' Her words passed through a thick bubble in her throat.

'Well, if it's not punishment, it feels close enough to the real thing.'

'This isn't a punishment, it's simply a fact of life. We accept that certain conditions naturally exist, so we have to accept this.' Her lips moved in a helpless fashion when she spoke.

'Don't be so reasonable. Certain conditions exist, they say, as though that means it's nothing to worry about. But ask them for an answer! The doctor gave me a diagnosis, sure, but he couldn't give me an answer, and the not knowing is somehow worse.'

'There's nothing else for us to know now. It's completely natural for you to feel angry at misfortune, but you won't do yourself any favours in punishing yourself, or looking for an answer to something that simply is what it is.' The shrill words filled the copse and a pair of pigeons burst from the boughs overhead with a frantic slapping of heavy wings.

'Even if they could tell me, there's nothing I can do about it now anyway. But I feel like I lived too long without some regard for my longevity and now whatever longevity I had, or thought I had...' This thought he let go, as though he realised the certainty of its impotent conclusion and, as though suddenly agitated, he made for the path out of the glade and she quickly fell in behind him.

They exited through the hedge gap into the forecourts and stepped directly into the warpath of two small dogs, each pent up to its fullest aggression, snapping jagged snarls and yapping at the other, and each owner reeling them by their leash like fishermen hauling in a spirited catch. As quick as their altercation had begun, it was over again, and upon separating each dog immediately reassumed its gay demeanour, and both dogs and owners went on miraculously unfazed by the moment of chaos.

'We always said we'd get a dog,' she said. 'Maybe we could have two, or three.' Her voice was cajoling, she squeezed his hand in hers.

They circled the dog walkers and sunbathers on the green and they spoke of dog breeds and names for dogs, and their path led them to the far side of the glade, through the hedge gap on a short, dark path under the immense foliage. Midges glowed huge and yellow and darted from scattered beams of sunlight into the shade like fireflies; he scratched his neck where they bit him and he fanned them away before his face, but they seemed not to bother her, and she went on talking brightly.

They stepped out of the cool shade of the trees and into the scorching sunlight on the path through the middle of the hayfork. His face was sweating and red where he scratched at midge bites and he looked weary from the walking and talking, and the noise of children at play and dogs barking engulfed them. The sky billowed and throbbed as the sun climbed against it and he looked down at his feet in that spot on the hot tarmac path and said,

'The problem with dogs is that they die and then you have to bury them.'

She dropped his hand and took a step back as she seemed to take stock of the person who could choose so abysmally his words.

He had offended her, and he knew so, as he did not look up from his spot when spoke next, asking,

'Who will bury us?'

They left the park and continued along the walking path upriver, saying very little to each other. The interval between her chimes grew as she swayed along behind him, allowing the sunshine to warm her face, her puffy eyelids closed, her rash cheeks held up to the blue infinite, and her hands clasping one another as though she communed with some potential spirit.

He kept himself just a few steps ahead of her with his hands slumped in his pockets.

The White Cart Water was wide upriver and far beneath the bridge the channel was drawn low, and pools of stranded river water pocked the stone beach where every stone was smoothed round and lay like huge beads, all along the water's edge. The river emerged from a dark corridor of ancient trees and coursed along the banks at the old snuff mill, through the bridge's great sandstone vaults, and ran off under the flank of trees that towered over the river from the bluff.

'For how long, do you think, people have been walking over this bridge?'

'I don't know. Hundreds of years probably.'

'Imagine the foresight that must have required. Where do you even begin with something that has to stay standing for hundreds of years?'

'They wouldn't have gotten round to laying the first stone if they'd been concerned with that. Their sole concern must've been to just get the bridge built, day in day out, one stone at a time.'

'Aye, whether they felt like it or not.'

'Exactly. Every day that they woke up and the bridge wasn't finished they knew what to be getting on with.'

The tautness with which she had held her expression was long slackened; the exertion of her rational and reasonable faculties had kept her from giving any line to that which might have taken them both overboard. She gave a weak smile when she saw he held her in his eyes and then each gave the other a look of startling recognition as the sound of a thin quack emanated from below them.

The crash of water around the piers so echoed through the vaults that neither he nor she seemed scarcely sure they'd heard anything at all, but threw themselves to the stone parapet to see, placed like a little ornament on a flat bead far below, a mother mallard. Her plumage was mottled brown and her eyes were black stripes, and swimming in a small pool behind her was her perfect miniature. The tuft of downy feathers shook itself out of the water and trotted with little leathery feet to join its mother by her side. Her quack came again, and the duckling spun its lead-coloured beak at her with sharp attention. The mother did not so much as turn her head, as though she feared detection, or was detecting something herself.

'She's missing one of her babies,' she realised aloud from the parapet, and quickly pressed her fingers to her lips; her eyes skimmed instinctively back and forth the channel and downstream of the mother she spotted a wet tuft, alone against the current and struggling.

'It's there.' She pointed sharply to where the duckling was pedalling courageously against the flow to rejoin its mother, but still its mother was unmoving, and the duckling conceded yet more territory to the riffling water and the distance from its mother grew quickly.

He clasped the capstones of the parapet with bone white fingers, and she gripped his arm with both hands as they watched the duckling brave the course of the waters. The little tuft of brown and yellow further conceded the right of way to the current and allowed itself to be carried far away by the run, before it found a lateral channel in the back flow, across which it swam strongly, and quickly, to reach at last the stone bank. They each let go the breath they held. The duckling shook itself and strutted across the shore of shining beads to rejoin its sibling and mother and promptly filed in behind the two waiting, before all three set off into the channel in a quick little row.

She released her grip on his arm and stepped to the far end of the parapet to see after the ducks, but they had gone off already from that place and headed into whatever world awaited them.

From the stone bridge the pair turned about and retraced their walk downriver, matching the flow of the White Cart Water. They neared a pair of steel and concrete bridges, one gated and disused, the concrete anchor of which was visible through the cherry laurels on the upland riverbank. The water level was only inches shy of the concrete ledge, which was bare and dry in the hot day.

He halted her with both hands, and with hushed awe in his face, he turned her and pointed through the screen of branches to the concrete ledge onto which, with an effortless dive from the river, and a calmness matching that of the waters from which it emerged, a riverine otter boar bounded slick and lithe. Its wet fur was like crude oil and its long upper body was overfired by its huge hind and so moved in tight circles like a wheelbarrow before couching itself at the edge, its long tail hanging off the plateau as if feeling for fine movement in the water. It's nostrils and ears popped open on its round head and its eyes shone black.

Her eyes were huge and bright, and joy seeped from her smile in a high whine; he raised a finger to his lip, but he did not shush her.

Then its ears tucked back into its fur and the boar was gone; its probing having raised issue from below the surface, it dripped from the ledge like a viscous gob clean through the water. The silty river held the boar's dark shape for a few long seconds before it pounced back onto the bridge anchor, and he saw the elation in her face at the boar's reemergence. They crept giddy as children to the neighbouring bridge to better see that the boar's fur was chestnut, its whiskers were white in the sun, its long underbelly was pale and they saw, hanging from the boar's mouth the sun-blind flesh of a minnow, its lustre shimmering like a prize as it flailed desperately in the summer air.

With its forepaws the boar pinned the spasming fish to the concrete and from under its wet nose, it sprouted a saw of white teeth and commenced consuming the catch headfirst. They watched in awe as the boar rent the fish of its eyes and head with gratified endeavour, whilst others who crossed the bridge did not care to stop and see the pale chin hairs peek through slivers of pink flesh and grape-coloured organs, nor to see that even halfway consumed the polished tail of the fish flailed on.

For the full course of its meal, the boar's tail securely probed the slow passing water and when its meal was finished, the boar went below the surface again with a clean ripple and reemerged with its mouth empty. Circling again the plateau and finding it unsatisfactory, the boar dripped off the ledge and swam on, leaving a clean and shimmering vee in its wake and was gone from their sight.

They watched the water and waited for the boar to reappear, but it never did. They looked down the river and saw the river was empty. They saw no otter, no fish, no ducks, but the ducks are there, somewhere, and there is a whole life in knowing that the ducks are there.

Gloria by David Stakes

In the summer of 1963, the 18-year-old Van Morrison was touring Germany with the Irish showband the Monarchs. It was there he wrote the song "Gloria," "one of the most perfect rock anthems known to humankind." It is a celebration of juvenile lust that belies its religious title.

It was recorded at Decca Three Studios in West Hampstead by his band, The Them on 5th April 1964. It was released on the B side of "Baby Please Don't Go." It is a song that lends itself to adaptation, improvisation, and extemporisation. This has led over the years to numerous interpretations from music greats like John Lee Hooker, Jim Morrison, and Patti Smith. Rooted in the Ulster Scots and Celtic heritage of its composer, it is part of Van's stream of consciousness; a stream that over the years has seeped into bars, tenements and loves of the Southside. The following is a humble celebration of that astral phenomenon.

(In the spirit of adaptation, the piece ends with some words from the Lyle Lovett song, "North Dakota" – "And I drank myself some whisky and dreamed I was a cowboy.")

In the humid summer's night,
She is walking down my street asking to take my hand.
A couple share cigarettes and glances outside Heraghty's Bar.
Who knows if they are fighting or loving.
A drinker cries, anyway love will only take you so far.
She wants to hold my hand to the sound of the Belfast cowboy on a radio,

She wants to get me to the close door,
The close where the Pride Flag hangs from the third floor.
And a joyous crowd of passers bye, say bring it all home,
Bring it home one more time.
They lure a drummer and a wastrel on the saxophone,
Saying someone like you can lighten the load.
Something about the banshees and the spirits of Sean and Sinead,
The distant lapping of Port Appin shore,
John Doherty and the diaspora of Donegall,
The queer folk of the Shaws.

A half-forgotten song, Jelly Roll Morton and the touch of soul.
The chanter calls for parting glass,
The constant beauty of Emmylou Harris.
Give me the certainty of the religious classes.
I want go back to the valley before the shadows fall,
Be closer to it all.
I want a last pint with Christy Moore,
Tell tales of Lisdoonvarna,
The little chapel at the Bridge of Orchy.
Thinking you need to take me to the Baptist church in the morning,
Because I'm tired of yearning.
I'm Thinking of total submersion.
But you take me by the hand and say
Let's look in the bookshop window,
See all our fictions and reflections.
Let's hang about the Roma Street corners,
Like the lads from the Salford Boys Club.
Torrisdale Street is tattooed on us,
The polished banister, the sandstone and ceramics.
All the walls in your house tell tall tales of Alisdair Gray,
A mural of Scottish factions
Paulo Nutini and his Dad's Italian café

Ivor Cutler and his harmonium
Jimmy Boyle and the Bar L pandemonium.
We can still stand where your bench was stolen.
A lucky lottery card will give us all we need,
For love, after all, is a greed.
So "take me down to the burning ground."

A lone doo descends on the neon light above Queen's Park Station.
Thoughts of you and the madness of our creation,
The complexities, the frustrations.
James Kelman and his greyhound breakfast
Janice Galloway and Clara Schumann
Jackie Kay and Bessie Smith.
I'm just looking for the words to give.
There is no hour too late for living.
Now you're walking down my street,
Wearing that little red dress
And there is still no let-up in the summer heat.
Echoes of stumbling heels on stone stairs.
You're knockin at my door.
Wont you let me in,
Gonna just let me in.
I want to hold your hand.
But I don't even know where to find the hall light.
You keep knocking at my door
In a little red dress.
And when you come in you say,
If you love me, say, "I love you".
If you love me take my hand.
If you love me, say, "I love you".
If you love me take my hand.
And you say "I love you",
And I give you my hand.

A DAY AT THE SEASIDE by Alex Meikle

It was good to get out of Glasgow, especially on a day like this. As the car sped up Battlefield Road approaching Shawlands on the way to the M77 and a speedy exit from the city, Steve reflected on what a beautiful morning this was and felt great for the first time in months.

It'd been a terrible year. Back in March, a routine health check had revealed a dodgy lump in a sensitive area. He'd been referred for a biopsy which came back positive for lymphoma. In plain terms, he had cancer of the lymph. A subsequent all-body PET scan revealed five tumours, though, crucially, none of them were in any of his vital organs.

Since then, he'd had four bouts of chemo at the world renowned Beatson Centre with no side-effects, which he was incredibly grateful for. There were two more to go and the prognosis was good; a recent PET scan revealed he was in "remission", basically the tumours had shrunk significantly; the chemo was working.

So, he had a lot to be thankful for: his treatment was working. He was in the best of hands and, courtesy of the much-maligned NHS, it was all free. Steve considered how, if he'd been living in the US, the costs would have wiped him out.

Back in Glasgow, he knew his savings would be untouched and thanks to his laptop and zoom, he could continue earning income from his consultancy on the days he didn't feel too fatigued. Though he was in his mid-sixties and officially "retired", he kept his hand in and made a reasonable living online and from his writing.

Tomorrow he was back at the Beatson for his fifth chemo session. For the next fortnight, he would be confined to his comfortable Battlefield flat, as his immune system would be low because of the chemo and his risk of infection high. So, today his friend, Ian was driving him down to the Ayrshire coast for Steve's last day out for a while.

For his part Ian thought they'd chosen the day well, as they hit the M77 and drove through the city's suburbs. It was late July, but it had been a miserable summer and the forecast for the coming weekend was for overcast skies and occasional showers. Ian was a teacher and in less than two weeks he'd be back at school; it really did look like the summer holidays would be a washout. Like his friend, Ian felt good to be going down to the coast on this one beautiful day.

But Ian was also immensely pleased to be driving his friend for a day out. Steve was a vibrant, confident, lively guy and the news he had the big C, which seemed to come out of nowhere, was shocking and profoundly depressing. Thankfully, Steve hadn't descended into dejection and despair; if anything, the opposite. He was stoical about the cancer; it was what it was, and he'd place himself in the hands of the medical staff in one of the world's best cancer treatment centres, which was on his doorstep. Nor had it dented his sense of humour, particularly Steve's dreadful "dad" jokes and awful puns, and he wasn't afraid to talk about the beastie, which gave Ian and his friends space to also talk about it and lighten up.

As they hurtled through the Ayrshire countryside, looking verdant in the sun, they exchanged banter, early Pink Floyd with Syd Barrett's distinctive vocals and quirky psychedelia from the car's sound system providing a nice background to their chatter. Traffic was light and they made good progress.

By just after eleven, they'd reached their destination. Girvan was over fifty miles from Glasgow, and they found a convenient parking spot not far from the beachfront. Like most towns on what had been termed the "Costa Clyde", Girvan had been a thriving destination for day trippers and longer-term visitors from Glasgow in days gone by. Those days were definitely in the past, as Steve and Ian ambled their way through the one main street. Though pleasant and clean, the town looked slightly run down and almost all the people around them seemed to be locals. As with most town centres in an online age, the main drag had plenty of empty shops and for sale signs.

They found a café with a bunch of friendly waitresses and Steve indulged in his usual high-jinks declaring that he was Ian's 'probation officer' and was accompanying Ian on an 'acclimatisation to civilian life exercise' which involved a day release' as he was coming to the 'end of a long custodial sentence' ('mind you it was nothing too violent, I can *assure* you, and he's got a tag on, so don't worry and he'll be taking his anti-psychotic pills in the next half-hour').

Ian was accustomed to this and just absorbed it while the waitering staff, God bless them, patently didn't believe him but went along and indulged him. Finally, they ordered soups and rolls and relaxed in the friendly, basic but homely ambience of the café.

Neither Steve nor Ian – who was in his mid-fifties- had ever married or had children. Both had had relationships but nothing too long-term. Though they often spoke about relationships and "settling down", both were confirmed bachelors who'd probably stayed single for too long to be comfortable, living with anyone else. That didn't prevent either from having close female friends, but they were strictly platonic, and it had been some years since they'd had a relationship that went beyond that.

But that didn't stop them speculating or fantasising. Two women came into the café, both in their late forties (an 'appropriate target age' as they put it to each other), one blond and the other with reddish-fair hair, slim and attractive. Immediately the two slipped into late middle-age male teenage adolescence mode and made furtive glances towards the women sitting across the way.

'Would you?' Steve asked.

'Definitely,' Ian concurred.

'I'd go for the redhead,' Steve said.

'The blonde's tidy,' Ian remarked. Both looked away quickly when the two women looked over.

It was pure fantasy and the arrival of their soup and rolls diverted them to their lunch. Halfway through, the two women left the café with not a glance in their direction.

'They obviously didn't want to fall out with each other over which of us they fancied the most,' Steve commented drolly. Ian grunted his agreement over his soup. Both knew this was absolute rubbish, but they enjoyed playing this game anyway.

Later, after finishing their lunch and paying the bill, they walked the short distance to the beachfront. It was a spectacular sight with a clear blue sky above them, lending a startling clarity to the view from the shore. They could clearly see the sheer cliff face of the isolated Ailsa Craig, more colloquially called "Paddy's Milestone" as it was alleged to be halfway to Ireland. Now uninhabited, it was a protected bird and wildlife sanctuary. Across the seascape was the vague outline of the low hills of the Mull of Kintyre and to their north the majestic grandeur of the Isle of Arran, with its landscape varying from gentle farmland and hills in the south of the island, building up to the formidable mountains in the north, climaxing at Goat Fell, which could even be seen on a clear day from Glasgow.

They drank in the view, before Steve declared that he felt tired, the effects of the treatment, even after just a short walk. They found a bench to sit on beneath and beside a stone wall, almost a palisade topped off by a grass park. From the bench they continued to stare out to sea, both happy and contented and certainly taking Steve's mind off the next day's chemo session.

'It's fantastic, isn't it?' Steve said taking it in.

'Sure is,' agreed Ian, trying not to think about going back to school in a few weeks.

'It's true what they say,'Steve continued, 'on a day like this, nothing can beat Scotland.'

'Agreed.' Ian's attention was taken up by a low thrumming hum in the distance. He looked up and saw a large silvery-grey aircraft coming in over the sea and rapidly approaching them. It had one long, continuous wing with four dark engines, two each suspended from either end of the wing and two smaller wings at the tail with the rudder and elevator above. It was quite a sight and very distinct from a normal passenger aircraft. Steve saw what had caused Ian's attention.

'That's a Lockheed C130 Hercules coming in,' Steve explained. 'It's military, US Airforce most likely and almost certainly heading to Prestwick.'

Prestwick was an international airport some thirty miles from Glasgow and not to be confused with that city's own airport. Though a few civilian airlines flew from Prestwick, most of its traffic was freight or, as in this case, military.

The plane flew directly overhead beginning to make a descent, and Steve couldn't help feeling an immense wave of satisfaction wash over him as they could clearly see the plane's markings including the words *United States Airforce* emblazoned on its fuselage.

As it passed over, Ian turned to Steve:

'Spot on Professor. You called that right.'

Steve shrugged his shoulders. 'I'm not just a pretty face mate.'

'Aye, whatever.'

The sound of the C130 began to fade as Steve went on:

'You know some pretty scary stuff went on at Prestwick back about twenty years ago just after 9/11.'

Ian nodded his head and was only too aware this was the prelude to one of Steve's "lectures". He was a very well-read man on a range of subjects and at times these could be genuinely enlightening and informative. At other times, though, they could be tedious, didactic and at times morphing into mansplaining. Ian prepared himself, as he didn't know which this would be.

'Aye, a lot of those big military transports were used by the yanks to, what they called "offshore" suspected al Qaeda operatives. They, the CIA say or any one of those three-letter agencies that make up the US intelligence community, would pick them up in one country and fly them to another country outwith US jurisdiction, such as Egypt or one of the central American states, and basically torture them, you know waterboard them and all that, before they took them back to the states for trial, or just to be incarcerated indefinitely in an orange jumpsuit at Guantanamo in Cuba.

'They called it extraordinary rendition and Prestwick was used as a refuelling base, while the suspects were kept blindfolded and hooded on board. The UK authorities turned a blind eye to it and the yanks denied it, of course, but there was plenty of good evidence it was going on. For example, a report from...'

Steve was warming to his theme now. He was looking away in the middle distance as he expounded and marshalled his thoughts, finger jabbing and gesticulating in the air. Ian knew this might last for another ten minutes, but the sight of his animated gestures could be quite entertaining.

'...a group of US Defence lawyers based on reports compiled from air traffic control logs in a range of...' Suddenly, he broke off.

Ian looked at him. Steve was transfixed, a quizzical look on his face.

'Do you hear that?' he asked. 'That noise, that high-pitched whine?'

At first Ian heard nothing. Then, as Steve had described, there was a high-pitched whine which was getting steadily louder. 'Yeah, I do,' Ian said.

They both looked up, but there was no aircraft to be seen in the cloudless sky.

'It's another military aircraft,' Steve declared authoritatively, craning his neck and scanning the sky in all directions. 'It's possibly a spy plane coming in low to avoid trackers. Yeah, there's still loads of dodgy things happening at Prestwick. We'll probably see it at the last minute.'

The noise was getting louder, but they could still see nothing.

'Those pilots are good at banking in low. Listen, that's definitely a US military jet engine. They're so distinctive. It's either a Prat and Whitny, or a GE or a Lockheed Martin. But definitely US Airforce again. Must be some clandestine military exercise going on.'

They were both now scanning the skies. Suddenly, the high-pitched whine cut out, then resumed, cut out again, resumed, cut out and resumed. Ian looked anxiously at Steve.

'Is he in trouble? Seems like the engine's cutting out.'

'Aye, you're right, but where is he?'

The whine was getting closer, but to Ian's surprise no one else on the beach or the promenade: families, couples, dogwalkers, seemed to take any notice.

Yet again, the engine seemed to cut out momentarily then restart. It was getting closer, almost above them.

Ian and Steven were now both spooked, convinced a US jet fighter aircraft was about to fall out of the sky and land on this Ayrshire seaside town with catastrophic consequences.

The noise was now deafening. Ian stood up. He looked at the stone bank directly behind their bench and at the grass lawn above it. And there was the "craft" in all its glory.

Only it wasn't a US jet fighter with serious engine trouble, but a mini electric council lawnmower truck weaving, cutting and mowing its way across the grass bank. The "pilot" was a council worker with a droopy moustache and a visible lanyard. Occasionally, the engine would stutter or cut out as the lawnmower met some resistance or obstacle and the driver would restart the engine.

'It's a fucking lawnmower!' Ian looked down at Steve, still on the bench.

'What?' Then he too looked up and saw the municipal vehicle at the edge of the grass verge. Steve looked crestfallen.

Of course, everybody else around knew what the sound was, had paid it no attention and got on with their business enjoying the sun, sea and view. All, except Ian and Steve, caught up in a doom loop spiral of military aircraft, jet engines, conspiracy and a stricken jet fighter about to plunge out of the skies.

Ian shook his head, still standing and brought out his mobile.

'I wish to God, I'd recorded you on my phone,' he said regretfully. 'That was classic, absolute classic. I could have put it on YouTube. Folk would have paid to see that. You rabbiting on, "*oh it's a jet fighter, listen that's a so and so engine*," then the bloody lawnmower van materialises with the wee guy driving it! Priceless. Come on let's get a walk and an ice cream.'

'Aye, all right,' Steve said dejectedly, rising from the bench.

Later, in the car heading home to the sound of Kate Bush's *Big Sky*, played deliberately by Ian, Steve pleaded:

'Between us eh, no need for anybody else to know about the lawnmower thing?'

Ian shook his head. 'Come on Steve, if it was the other way around, you'd slag me remorselessly. There's just *no* way I could not tell this.'

'Aye, I know,' Steve conceded.

Ian knew Steve had the ability to laugh at himself and if Ian didn't mention the "lawnmower incident" as he was beginning to frame it, Steve would.

As they passed by a clutch of houses to their left, they saw a chap working on his garden. Ian said,

'Aye, it's a lovely day for the garden, get the lawnmower out, just make sure you don't mistake it for a spy plane.'

'That's it started, has it?' Steve asked.

Ian shook his head and almost whispered: '*Aye.*'

'Ok,' Steve said,' 'I'll tell the nurses at the Beatson tomorrow during chemo; they should enjoy the laugh.'

They drove onto Glasgow. It'd been a good day at the seaside.

The Queen of the Shaws by Laura McPherson

The soft white fur that surrounds her wee nose
Sniffs the fresh air through the crack in the window
Her Kingdom is the Birness Flats
Pale green eyes examining her subjects below
The Queen rules over the dominion of the Shaws

Sniff, sniff, sniff
The Queen tilts her head
Golden blank discs stare back at her
He is not like me,
A companion chosen by the Guardians that I merely tolerate.

Pad, pad, pad, a flash of black and white joins her
The trill sounded by her companion
As the birds circle overhead
Perhaps I will come back as a pigeon
Fly over the territory that borders my own

The Guardians call this The New Lands
And the realm of Pollok
Where the Legend of the Red Flamed Coo resides
A chirrup, blank eyes bore into her own
I'll need to take him with me
Not without a swat of my paw
I may have to spend eternity with you
But Be Gone from my Throne!

She slowly lays down, resembling a freshly baked loaf
Her eyes narrow into slits,

The sun is warm today.

An Heir must be found
Perhaps a small kitten with fur like midnight will suffice
Yes, Little One, our Regions will widen
The Shaw Lands will be yours
And over the Hill
Where Legend goes another Great Queen passed through

I will take my eternal form, when your turn comes to pass
Little One, I will guide you
With a gentle coo from your window ledge
My wings will soar through the realm of the Shaws
Just like that Blue Butterfly, I will ascend

The sun is warm today

Sincerity is jiggery-pokery by Hugh V. McLachlan

Several years ago, my elderly friend, Victor Tonkin, suggested on the phone that we visited Pollok House, a very grand property, which was designed by William Adam. It lies in Pollok Country Park, about three miles or so from Victor's home in the Southside of Glasgow. He recommended highly the paintings which were on display. He mentioned too that there was some sort of interesting astronomical clock there which showed the signs of the zodiac, the position of the sun, the phases of the moon, the water level at high and low tide as well as telling the time. It was made, he said, around 1746. As an afterthought, he said that it would make an interesting comparison with his Apple Watch.

Victor has an Apple Watch! I could not believe it. They were a novelty then. They were cutting edge. I was amazed that he had even heard of them. However, he assured me that he had one. He said that he was wearing it as we spoke.

Victor is retired now from his job as an academic. He was still working then. I had not known him very long at the time. The measure of the man still eluded me. He was fascinating. He seemed to me to be clever and insightful but, often, incomprehensible and irritating. He was, sometimes, cogent and concise. He was, sometimes, rambling and obscure.

What, I wonder now, did he think of me then? How obtuse I must have seemed! How humourless and over-earnest.

We arranged to meet at the entrance of Pollok House, where he would show 'the ticking timepiece', as he called it, to me. On the phone, he called me – Alexander 'Sandy' Beecham – a 'doubting Thomas'.

'But', I said, 'Doubting Thomasism is the only possible rational attitude to have, is it not? It is the scientific approach, surely'.

'It depends,' he said, 'it depends what you mean by "Doubting Thomasism". It is rational, in general, to want to have evidence for theories before you are prepared to confidently maintain that they are true. However, it is not rational to accept only the evidence which you have acquired directly with your own eyes. Science would not have progressed from one generation to the next if all scientists had started from scratch at birth with a *tabula rasa* – a blank slate – and filled it in as their own experience of witnessing the evidence for particular scientific theories accumulated.

'It is rational to say that you are not prepared to believe that, for instance, there is a monster in Loch Ness unless you are presented with good evidence. However, if you were presented with good evidence, it would be whimsical, it would be pig-headed to insist that you would refuse to believe such a monster existed until you had actually seen it in person with you own eyes.'

'Strange things happen, Sandy. Unbelievable things happen. To refuse to believe in the occurrence of any particular thing as a matter of some supposed philosophical principle because you did not witness that thing yourself would be crazy.'

'Maybe so', I said 'But I still want to see the watch'.

He is not a luddite. He does not disapprove of technological advances as such - not, at least, when he gets used to them. But an Apple Watch? It was difficult to imagine him wearing such a thing. He is, to say the least, no slave to fashion. He does not think that the latest is the best. When people say, as some of them sometimes do, that some opinion or, say, some policy or other is 'on the right side of history', he is very dismissive of their view. There is no inevitable evolutionary progress in language or any other social conventions, laws and institutions. So he maintains. In some respects, some things might happen to get better. In some respects, some things might happen to get worse. History is multi-directional. It is not committed to any particular side or direction.

'People,' he says, 'used to talk about guys and dolls and guys and gals. Now, everyone is a guy, according to some people.' Victor does not approve. 'Call my wife a "guy", Sandy, and I will call you an ambulance.' He was smiling when he once said this to me, but I took the hint and never called Mary a 'guy' again.

Mary Gonzalez, also known - if and when, for her own purposes, Mary chooses – as Mary Gonzalez-Tonkin or Mary Tonkin is Victor's second wife. Mary and Victor had a son who died in childhood. If he had lived, he would be around the age that I am.

Mary is an actuary. Being an actuary, Victor says, means 'Doing a lot of hard sums for a lot of hard cash.' She earned much more than he did. Mary is extremely good at doing crosswords. Victor says that he hides his 'Times' from her in the morning since, otherwise, she will have finished the crossword before he has had a change to try to start it.

Victor can get particularly annoyed about what he considers to be changes for the worse in the use of words. For instance, he says that, in his day, 'misogyny' meant 'hatred of women' but that nowadays the word can refer to any attitude or behaviour towards women which the user of the word happens to object to. 'Not all such so-called "misogyny" is wrong' he says, 'and not all wrong attitudes and wrong forms of behaviour towards women are misogynistic.'

He says: 'It is wrong, say, to wolf-whistle at women in the street – it is, among other wrong things, rude and disrespectful - but it is not necessarily an expression of or an outcome of hatred of women.'

Clarity of thought and expression are not furthered by what Victor considers to be this extension of the meaning of the word 'misogyny'.

He can rant enthusiastically about for instance, the words 'homophobia', 'Islamophobia' and 'transphobia'. According to Victor, they are clear examples of words that stifle debate and generate befuddlement. He points out that phobias are medical conditions. If people are suffering from a phobia about, for instance, homosexual people or homosexuality, we should be sympathetic towards them, and be prepared to offer them any available help and treatment. We should not blame them or castigate them any more than we should criticise someone who has, for instance, influenza or a morbid fear of and anxiety about spiders.

If people do not suffer from a relevant medical condition, we should not apply what sounds like a medical term to their views. We should not call people 'homophobes' or 'Islamophobes' or 'transphobes' merely because we disagree with what they think, or because we find their views repugnant. We should not use an apparent medicalisation of their position as an excuse for failing to consider their arguments.

Not all people who have objections to, for instance, the legalised self-identification of gender status will hate or, even, dislike gender transition or transgender people. Those who do have such hatreds or dislikes will not necessarily have transphobia. Not all hatreds and dislikes are medical conditions. In any case, whether an argument is a good one and whether the person who puts it forward is a good person are quite separate questions. Good arguments can be presented by bad people for dubious motives. So Victor likes to insist.

Similarly, good people with good intentions can put forward bad arguments and can believe ridiculously false things.

Victor is a fan of George Orwell. Apparently, he wrote his famous book '1984' in Scotland, on the island of Jura. As is well known, in that book, Orwell writes about 'Newspeak', which is designed to diminish the range of thought by such things as inverting and perverting the customary meanings of words. Thus, in the book, 'Big Brother' - the euphemism for the unbrotherly state - bombards the public with propagandist slogans such as: 'War is Peace'; 'Freedom is Slavery'; 'Ignorance is Strength.'

According to Victor, Orwell also wrote an essay called 'Politics and the English Language'. The book and the essay both illustrate Orwell's view, that there is a reciprocal relationship between language and politics. Corrupt thought can lead to a degeneration of language which, in turn, has a corrupting effect on subsequent thought, in Orwell's view.

I have often heard Victor quoting Orwell's claim that: 'The great enemy of clear language is insincerity. When there is a gap between one's real and one's declared aims …'. According to Orwell, when politicians are others are insincere, and there is a gap between their latent and their manifest aims, they tend to resort: 'to long words and exhausted idioms, like a cuttlefish spurting out ink.'

Staleness of imagery and lack of precision are features which Orwell associates in particular with the use of tired, carelessly used metaphors. One of his suggested rules of writing is: 'Never use a metaphor, simile, or other figure of speech which you are used to seeing in print.' This is asking a lot, a hell of a lot, of any writer, in my view.

In this regard, Victor argues that we should be suspicious of such clichés as 'control of the levers of power' and 'level playing field'. They add little if anything to our understanding and explanation of the issues in question. They can be positively misleading, he says.

States, societies and economies are not like ships or vehicles that can be controlled and directed mechanically by the manipulation of accelerators, brakes and steering wheels.

Politicians can exercise authority. They can pass laws. They can formulate and implement policies. By their strategies, they can have effects on the economies and on other institutions of the countries in which they have political jurisdiction, but causation is not the same as control. Societies and economies are not directly controlled by their politicians although they are to an extent affected by them. They, the societies and economies, are also affected by a host of other things including the policies, decisions and strategies of the politicians of other states. Moreover, consciously or unconsciously, citizens can and often do alter their behaviour in reaction to the laws and policies which politicians introduce in ways which they do not predict, intend or want.

Hibernian Football Club used to have a non-level playing field. This was the famous Easter Road Slope. That did not preclude the possibility of fair and equal contests there. The teams change ends at half-time.

In a sprint, in a marathon and in a foot race of any sort, able-bodied males would tend to win if the track on which they all ran were a level one. If able-bodied male runners had rough, uneven and undulating tracks while the other competitors had smooth, even, level ones, an equality of outcomes between them would be less unlikely. If all runners had rough, uneven and undulating tracks, there would be a greater chance of random falls and stumbles and this too would be of assistance to the less able runners. Fluke results, although unlikely, would be less unlikely. Hence, the metaphor of a level playing field can hardly help to illustrate or explain why in various other non-athletic spheres or life, women and disabled people tend to be under-represented in the higher-ranking positions.

Victor is not a climate change denier, far from it. However, he dislikes the tactics and the arguments of eco-warriors. He even dislikes the arguments and language that is normally used with regard to climate change.

For instance, Victor argues as follows. He says that we might assume, for the sake of the argument, that syphilis is a problem and that it is caused by sexual intercourse. It does not follow that the solution of the problem must be the reduction, far less the elimination of sexual intercourse. No, there is another, better solution: penicillin.

Similarly, he argues, climate change is a problem of which the emission of greenhouse gases is the cause or at least, a central cause. A reduction in the emission of such gases would mitigate the problem. Their elimination might solve it. However, it does not follow that their elimination is the only possible solution, or that it is necessarily the best solution. Whether or not there might be one practical solution, analogous to penicillin with regard to syphilis, there might be a number of partial analogous practical, technological solutions which in combination with a reduction, even if not the total elimination of greenhouse gases, will solve the problem.

We should not rely totally on the discovery of a solution analogous to penicillin, we should also try to reduce the elimination of greenhouse gases. But we should not rely totally on the elimination of greenhouse gases. We should also seek a mitigation of the problem in other ways. However, just as there are puritans who would much prefer the problem of syphilis to be solved by abstention from sex outside marriage, there are puritans of another sort who would prefer the problem of climate change to be solved, as far as possible, by the elimination of greenhouse gases. So Victor says.

Victor thinks that the word 'sustainable' has a damaging effect on the quality of public discussions of public policy.

'It's almost as if "sustainable" was another word for "good" and "unsustainable" another word for "bad", which is an absurdity', he says.

'An erection is not very sustainable, not for me, not these days' he says. 'It doesn't mean that it isn't worth having one. It does not make an erection a bad thing. There again, a permanent erection, one that would never become deflated, would be a hellish affliction. It would cause discomfort and embarrassment while you were alive and it would cause a problem for the undertaker to get the lid on your coffin when you were dead. '

'I am not convinced that 'sustainability' is a sensible or even a coherent notion. What you want is an erection which does not last for too long or for too short a time. Temporary permanence? No: temporary optimal viability. That's what we should be after.'

'Life is not sustainable indefinitely either for any individual human being or for the human race. The planet itself will not have an infinite duration. All we hope is that it will last for a very, very long time.'

He can go on and on for ages on this and his other contrarian opinions.

He says: 'I doubt if there ever has been or ever could be an economic system or, even, an economic activity which did not require the use of some resources, which were scarce in the sense that their supply was finite. I suspect that we can and should move from one unsustainable system on to another unsustainable system and so on until, eventually, the world becomes uninhabitable.'

'Suppose that someone had said, prior to the industrial revolution that it was unsustainable, because the potential supply of coal, on the power from the burning of which it would be fuelled, is finite. It would have been a great pity if, on that ground, the industrial revolution had been thwarted. The industrial revolution was, or approached, temporary optimal viability. That made it worthwhile until some other system which was not so reliant on coal became, temporarily, more optimal.'

'Temporary optimal viability or some such notion would seem to me to make more sense as a target than "sustainability". On the one hand, systems that were viable cease to be when finite resources become too scarce. On the other hand, changes in technology make novel systems viable even if only temporarily.'

Victor is not, in principle, against technology. On the other hand, in practice, he shows no great enthusiasm for particular technological devices. If Victor and I are ever in company with other people, he looks with disapproval at me if I scroll my phone. However, he has a mobile phone. I have never seen it, but I know he has one because I often phone him on his mobile phone number. But – an Apple watch? I couldn't imagine it.

I was looking forward to my coffee in the advertised Edwardian kitchen in Pollok House, which we planned to visit whenever Victor arrived. We were due to meet at quarter past eleven, but Victor has a habit of arriving very early for appointments of any sort. As it approached eleven o'clock, I wondered whether the astronomical clock inside the house would chime. 'Does it tick loudly?', I asked myself.

Then, it dawned on me - the obvious flaw in Victor's story of his Apple watch. Apple watches, surely, do not tick, yet he had referred to his watch as his 'ticking timepiece'. He had tried, again, to bamboozle me but, this time, he had failed. I resolved to confront him – 'call him out', as I might then have put it - as soon as he arrived.

'Pollok House is a cool place to be in, Sandy', said Victor when he appeared.

'Cool?', I said.

It is not a word that I had ever heard him use before. It sounded very strange coming from him.

'When I say that it is 'cool', I am referring solely to the objective measurement of the temperature inside the building', he said.

It turned out that he had walked all the way to Pollok House from his own house in what was a very warm day. Why didn't he get a taxi? He could well afford it. Why didn't he learn to drive?

'Did I ever tell you what is thought to be the origin of the notion of "cool"?' asked Victor. 'It comes, apparently, from American slavery ...'

I had to cut him short. Not an easy thing to do. His meandering patter was preventing me from revealing to Victor that his scheme to fool me over his supposed possession of an Apple watch had failed.

I said, sarcastically: 'The great enemy of clear language is insincerity'.

He butted in by saying: 'When there is a gap between one's real and one's declared aims?'.

I almost swore, but I composed myself and told him that he was lying when he said he owned an Apple watch and also explained how I had rumbled him.

'Don't you want to see it?' he said. He thrust his hand, with an open palm, towards me.

'No, Victor', I said. 'I refuse to look. Whatever I might see upon your wrist, I refuse to believe it is an Apple watch'.

Victor laughed. 'That sounds almost biblical', he said. 'And very unscientific'.

'How can you say, in all sincerity, that you are wearing an Apple watch?', I said.

He said: 'I can and do sincerely say that I am wearing what I call my "apple watch."'

I was flummoxed.

He continued: 'My wife and I often listen to the wireless together. We like to listen to "The Archers" in the evening on the BBC, on Radio 4.'

'What does that have to do with anything?', I snapped, impatiently.

Looking at his watch, he said: 'I set it by the pips.'

I groaned. I groaned, if Orwell would approve, like a bin lorry grinding to a halt in a gravel pit.

Tartan Dreams by Alan Gillespie

Choose football. Choose your country. Choose
singing out loud.
Choose tartan trousers, choose a Glengarry, painted faces,
Retro shirts and the Hampden roar.
Choose own goals, getting humped, bleak tears of frustration.
Choose a big plate of currywurst for your breakfast.
Choose dancing in the streets under blue saltire skies.
Choose bumping into old school pals in the departure lounge.
Choose Lorraine Kelly on your morning telly.
Choose telling your children things used to be worse,
We've lifted the curse.
Choose the kilt your grandfather wore on his wedding day.
Choose Flower of Scotland getting stuck in your skull.
Choose tartan dreams in your lion rampant sheets.
Choose taking the high road. Choose meeting your true love
Once again, on the bonnie, bonnie banks.
Choose riding a unicorn. Swimming with Nessie. Bouquets of
thistles.
Choose partying away at the final whistle,
Bursting for the toilet on foreign soil, showing the world
That *we* are the sons and daughters of Scotland,
And they will hear us coming, coming down the road.

La Signora Sweeney by Barney MacFarlane

SHE was one dumb cluck. Even received wisdom seemed to have passed her by. It annoyed her, embarrassed her that a second-generation Italian, such as herself, could not speak Italian.

And her name – Anastasia Sweeney. What kind of a handle was that? She should never have married that pisspot stumer Patsy. Well rid of him, certainly. Took a bottle of Jameson's whiskey round to one of his navvy mates a couple of years back and she never saw him again. Suited her fine. Even the weans didnae miss him. Christ, they hardly knew him. He never knew them either. Any time he saw them in the morning, he couldnae remember their names!

But now as she sat in the empty house it annoyed her that she only knew a couple of words of Italian. Last week it didn't bother her so much. He – her father – had always tried to speak to her in his native tongue but each time she ignored him.

"Look Daddy, this isnae Naples," she would moan. "This is Glesca. The only folk that speak Italian here are Tallies. If you want to speak Italian go tae the Casa."

The Casa was a club used by the Italian community in the city.

"Ma tu sei Italiana." He attempted once more to appraise her of her roots. She ignored him again.

Daddy would go off in the huff to listen to his Caruso records.

The Madonna and Baby Jesus stared at her from the picture on the wall. Ana did not have far to look for spiritual inspiration in that house, her parents' house. Religious paintings hung everywhere and if a shelf space had ever presented itself, an icon of a saint had promptly staked its claim. Today the living room was full of the heady perfume of flowers. Ana stood in the centre of the room. She was cloaked in black. Tall, still strong but feeling frail. Mortal.

The hubbub of voices approached. Ana walked into the narrow lobby and opened the door. Her mother Mary led a stream of black-clad mourners up the steps of the tenement.

"Oh, hello, hen," her mother greeted her, out of breath. "Kettle on?"

"Aye." Ana brushed away an imaginary speck of dust from the lapel of the jacket of her elder son, Sean who was holding on to his grandmother's elbow, as if she might collapse without his help.

"This daft boy o' yours, Ana," said Mary, taking off her coat. "Thinks I'm an auld wumman. I've goat a few good years in me yet, tell him."

The young man assumed a pained expression and joined his brother Mike in the kitchen, where the younger one was already nibbling a hot sausage roll, while eyeing up French cakes.

Later, after everyone had left, Ana stayed on to clear up. She and her mother had the place spotless within half an hour. They sat down, exhausted, each with a mug of tea. The china was back in the sideboard.

Ana looked at her mother. She seemed to be somewhat circumspect where grief was concerned as she puffed, apparently contentedly, on her fag and slurped her tea. Ana said, "I was just sittin' here earlier and thinkin' how stupid I was never to learn Italian."

Mary glanced up. "Well, don't look at me. I'm no' a bloody Tally. It was nothin' but trouble for me efter I met yer faither."

"How so?" Ana had never heard this confession before.

"From my Da'. He didnae like Tallies. It was jist efter the war, don't forget. Never forgave me." The old woman paused, examining the gold ring on her arthritic finger. "Ach, whit dae

I care? He was a miserable auld bastard, my faither. Bit like that balloon you married."

Ana frowned and then smiled. Her mother was right. As usual. "But," she continued on her earlier thought, "Daddy always wanted me to learn Italian and I would never do it. Now he's away and I feel as if I failed him."

"Ach, don't be so daft, hen. Whit's done is done. Nae use in worryin' aboot it. Christ, ye didnae care much aboot it when he wis livin'."

Just like her mother. Get straight to the point of pain. Ana said no more about it. She knew what she was going to do. She just wouldn't tell anyone. That was all.

Three weeks later, Ana attempted to squeeze her long legs into the space provided by the desk in front of her. The woman standing at the front of the class was about the same age as herself. She smiled. Ana smiled.

"Buona sera, signori e signore. And welcome to the Standard Grade Italian class here at Langside College. Don't know if you're aware but – assuming you all pass, ha ha – you'll be the last group to have gained the certificate at evening class here. Because of financial cutbacks and falling rolls, they're closing the college down."

God, it was my last chance, thought Ana. It must have been meant.

The lecturer started to chalk a name on the blackboard then turned to face the class. "That's me," she said, pointing to the words. "Valentina McSwegan. Horrendous juxtaposition, isn't it? Well, that's what happens when a second generation Italian marries a Glasgow bloke."

Ana smiled again and thought language a wonderful thing. She whispered to herself – *Plus ca change, plus c'est la meme chose.*

But that was another story.

The Round by J D Allan

When I was sixteen, I had a brief stint as an Air Cadet. Glossy recruitment posters of de Havilland Chipmunks and open-cockpit gliders found their quarry. My local squadron was headquartered in an old drill hall in Pollokshaws on the south side of Glasgow. After weeks of parading about, I was bored silly. Emblazoned on our squadron's crest was the Air Training Corps' motto: "Venture, Adventure". *Lies*, thought I. Finally, it came time for my first proper cadet activity: target shooting. Following some rudimentary instruction, I was handed a World War II-era rifle and five .22 calibre rounds. I decided to keep a round as a souvenir and planked one in my left trouser pocket. From the prone position, we fired at targets of charging cartoon squaddies, like so many panels I'd seen in Commando comics. After we had exhausted our ammunition, an NCO ordered us to fall in.

'As per the Firearms Act 1968, it is an offence to be in possession of live rounds without holding a firearm certificate. Do any of you hold a firearm certificate?'

'NO, FLIGHT SERGEANT!' came the synchronous reply.

'Very well. You will now be searched.' Panic clamped me. 'I want you to place your left hand into the right trouser pocket of the cadet to your left and call out if you find any rounds.' Perplexed silence. 'Do you understand?'

'YES, FLIGHT SERGEANT!' We did as instructed. While shifting back into position, I slipped my left hand into my left trouser pocket and palmed the round. Icy specks of sweat were germinating on my neck and temples.

'Now place your right hand into the left trouser pocket of the cadet to your right.' Again, we did as instructed. 'No call-outs. Splendid,' said the NCO, pulling at the seams on his breeks.

'Only one thing more. Hold out your hands in front of you, palms up.' The game was a bogey. I let the round drop. In slow motion, it sank away from me like a little submarine. When it hit the concrete floor, it rang out like a bell. Every head spun in my direction. For the avoidance of doubt, the round lay on the ground, pointing at me. In short order, I was in front of the squadron leader.

'This is very serious, cadet. What have you got to say for yourself?' I thought hard for a moment, and then it came to me.

'VENTURE ADVENTURE, SIR!' So ended my time in the Air Training Corps.

Tom by Sandy McGiven

Tom Banks crouched low and tight to the tree and looked down the embankment to the path below and waited.

A rush of wind blew through the trees and was welcomed by the leaves as they gave their static applause.

Tom moved.

Staying in a crouched position, he made his way through the undergrowth of the woodland, the sound of broken twigs and dry winter leaves hidden in the noise above. When the wind stopped, Tom stopped.

Looking down at the path he saw a woman in a bright red coat walking her dog, a Labrador, this may be a problem as the dog would smell him. The dog kept its nose to the ground, sniffing, then looked up towards the trees where Tom hid. The black dog looked up and stared directly at Tom for a second then moved on to the path ahead, the dog's owner none the wiser.

Tom watched the woman walk along the path in the opposite direction that he was moving. As Tom watched he also caught sight of who was coming towards her on the same path.

There was three of them. Two men and one woman. They always hunted in packs.

They were looking in all directions as they walked along the path. One of them, a middle-aged man, who looked like he could be in charge of the search, stopped the dog walker and started talking to her. Tom couldn't hear what was being said however it looked like he was asking her questions. The woman looked around and shook her head. Tom thought, "You haven't seen me. I'm too clever for you lot. Too fast, too strong, too young."

Another gust of wind came through the trees and Tom took advantage of his enemies caught in chat and moved again. This time he did not stop. He knew he was not far from Snuff Hill Bridge, just outside of Linn Park's woodlands. If he could get to the bridge hopefully Meredith would be there waiting for him.

Tom could remember the days when he too walked through the park with excited anticipation at meeting Meredith, she always stood on the left side of the bridge watching the water flow away from her. This always gave Tom the opportunity to creep up on her and give her a playful fright. On a Friday night after his shift at Weirs Pumps, he would meet her here and go straight to the Old Smiddy pub for drinks and they would catch up on each other's week. When Meredith turned round on the bridge her smile would take him by surprise every time, her red hair, bushy, bursting out of her beret hat.

Tom climbed up the embankment pulling at the undergrowth and ferns to help him. He was soon on the higher path that ran in parallel with the path down by the river that his enemies had taken. He started to speed up his walk to a slow run. He passed Holmwood House to his left and knew he was minutes away. Both paths meet before leaving the park for the bridge and Tom knew he had to beat them. Speed was of the essence however Tom knew he had youth on his side and leaned forward slightly picking up the pace even more. Soon Tom reached the point where both paths met, no one was there, he had beat them. Keep moving.

Tom slowed down as he looked over to his right towards the bridge. It's high arch and centre point empty of anyone, only the a subdued roar of the river flowing under it. It always flowed and would never end, just like us Meredith would tease.

Tom couldn't wait, he knew they would be close behind him. What should he do, hide close by for Meredith. Tom stood looking at the river for what seemed like an age. He turned and looked at the cobbled stones of the bridge and realised the rain was hitting off them. He touched his trousers then his hair and swept it back, soaked. Why hadn't he noticed the rain. Then it dawned on him. Meredith would be in the pub out of the rain. If it was raining she would always go on to the pub and wait for him. No time to waste. Tom's bare feet slapped the wet cobblestones as he ran down the other side of the bridge, looking round to check his chasers had not appeared from the woods. He then took a left and followed the road round until the pub was in front of him. A welcome sight where so many good nights had been had with Meredith and friends.

Tom pulled the pub door open and felt the warmth of the pub mixed with the sweet smell of beer and the background noise of people engaged in conversation. He stepped in and as the door closed behind him, he realised that some of the people close by were staring at him, looking him up and down. Could there be some of his enemies here as well? The barman's cry snapped him from his thoughts.

"Hey Tom, how are you, come in mate the weather is dismal, you ok?"

"Yes, yes" said Tom and instantly felt better for the barman's attention. He looked familiar however Tom could not remember his name.

" Have you seen Meredith ?" asked Tom

Now leaning against the bar and looking around trying not to act nervous. The barman would have no idea the situation he was in and the danger Meredith could be in.

" Eh no Tom I haven't, why don't you have a drink and wee seat and she might be along soon, what are you having mate?"

"Whisky please, neat" Tom put his hand in his pocket looking for his wallet when the barman just nodded and gave a friendly wink, "On me, Tom."

Tom took the glass and walked over to a small round table, there were two chairs. Sitting on the one nearest the wall, Tom would see Meredith coming in, and anyone else for that matter.

Tom sat patiently waiting for Meredith. Looking over at the bar he noticed the barman looking at him, he looked away quickly when Tom made eye contact. He then watched him go through the back door although, Tom could still see him reflected in an old mirrored whisky advert hanging to the side of the bar. Tom watched as he picked up a phone and started talking to someone. Tom started to get paranoid, not a bad thing to keep your wits about you in such situations. After a few minutes the barman reappeared and looked straight at Tom with what looked like a sympathetic smile. Tom knew something was not right. The barman's eyes shifted to the door and Tom's followed. The bar door opened and the two men from the park walked in. Tom knew what to do. Getting up quickly and with no great rush,he walked calmly further into the pub where a side door to the right brought you out to the side street. Tom was soon out. Tom then ran.

Getting out of the side lane of the pub, Tom made his way back to the park, heading for the bridge. The barman was one of them, bloody knew it. Trust no one.

Tom knew they wouldn't be long before they realised he was no longer in the pub and they would give chase.

As Tom came round the corner to see the bridge on his right, he could see a figure on the bridge. As he got closer his heart rate started to increase. It was Meredith. He knew that silhouette a mile away. She was looking at the river flowing away from her. She was standing slightly side on so he could not see her face and she could not see him coming.

Tom slowed down as he approached the bridge, Meredith only twenty feet away now. No time for games of surprise now, he had to get her away from here.

"Meredith, where have you been? We need to go. I'll explain everything. There are people after us. We need to move now."

At that point Meredith turned round and smiled, Tom stepped back. Shocked. It wasn't Meredith. It was the woman who was chasing him, the woman who was with the two men, she was old, her hair was grey, bushy, under a hat. She smiled and Tom looked at her teeth, a yellow shade with age.

Tom stumbled back, he suddenly felt the cold of the cobbled stones on his feet and the rain started to hit him, even the noise of the rain hitting the bridge, hitting him with rhythmic dull pats. As he stumbled, the old woman moved towards him, her arms outstretched. There was genuine concern in her face, she started to look familiar in some strange way.

Tom noticed the woman glance over his shoulder and Tom turned to see the two young men standing behind him.

He was surrounded. There was no escape.

Both men smiled, however not maliciously, again it seemed like concern. Tom started to feel sick as he knew something was wrong and didn't want to know the truth, he didn't know why.

" Dad, lets go home, you're soaking wet," said one of them.

He turned towards the woman who had taken a step closer.

"Yes Dad, lets go. Get a wee dram in the house to heat you up," said the other man, who appeared to be the younger of the two.

He turned again and the woman was closer again, he could feel her breath against his face and as she smiled with her arms outstretched, he took a step forward and embraced Meredith.

He hugged her and felt the warmth of someone he was in love with, had always been in love with and always would be. Standing on the bridge where they always met, and now even through the diseased labyrinth of dementia, his love always navigated him back to a safe place where love would always be there. Always flowing, just like the river, just as Meredith had said all those years ago.

As they slowly walked off the bridge towards a car, Tom gripped Meredith's hand and smiled at her, then quietly whispered.

" When I say run, you run and don't stop, I'll find you, let me take care of these two."

Musings On A Mat by Gillian Booth

It took me a long time to get here
No I don't mean here on my Pilates mat;
I have always been on it, or at least very near
I mean here in my mind, my breath and core.
No one understands when I talk about this, I sound like a bore
What is it about you that I cannot resist?
It's like a hold, so tight in a fist;
Even in the coldest Southside mornings, through a bad nights sleep
I always turn up, roll you out and begin without so much as a peep.
We have travelled the world together;
You are my map and I'm your guide
Though we know we are our happiest when we're home in Langside.
Accept it - I am yours for the next hour
Yes believe it! You really do have that much power;
Some days I cannot even touch my toes,
On others I strike an incredible pose!
If I am your biggest supporter
You're my harshest critic;
What is it that makes me keep coming back to you?
Is it because you promise me a beautiful body?
Or is it that I know without you I'll start to look shoddy?
The ebb and flow of movement on you is seductive I won't lie;
Concentration, centering, control, precision and breathing - I promise I will try….

Why do we keep up this practice?
You know me better than I know myself;
You can sense the worry in my head, by my side like an elf.
Everything is better when I'm on my mat,
Come on let's do the 100's - you'll have me purring like a cat!
Your four corners tell me it's all going to be ok.
Finally I come down into the rest pose like I am ready to pray;
I love it when it's just us, some candles and my favourite moves,
I can do anything with this body and the best bit is you won't disapprove.
I'm always here and you're always there
My beautiful mat, we make a perfect pair.

Trip to Scotland 2023 - Southside Memories by Daniel Ritchie

It was when they stood at the closed gates of Linn Park, on the cusp of the Snuffmill Bridge, that he finally realised he was home. The gate was locked because the pathway was dangerous, falling rocks from the cliff could pulverise you if you were unlucky. They had travelled a long way, the boys were now men, and Helena felt at home too. His knees were not as good as they used to be but he felt he could still make the riverside walk on the other side of the bridge. The sun was hotter now. Holmwood must surely still be there, his boys were stunned by the beauty of the place. He pointed out the house they had almost bought when they were still in their wild and crazy days. They began to cross the bridge, leaning over the walls and looking down on the Cart, sun sprinkling through the overhanging trees, the water's high marks on the walls of the houses on the bank.

So they crossed the bridge and entered the park, climbing up some steps before stepping onto the moss-covered earth path. Both sides of the path were covered by ancient trees, and most of the light had been blocked out. On their left, a solid wooden fence ran alongside the path and the earth sloped down to the river, without the fence someone could easily slip down the steep slope and end up in the water. After a bit, they noticed a black cat had begun silently following them. Helena stopped and began talking baby talk to it, and bent down to try and stroke it but the cat hissed at her and tried to scratch. They walked on laughing and joking. He told them stories of how when he was young we thought witches, warlocks, elves, fairies and all sorts of creatures lived on this side of the river.

They began to hear voices and laughter further up on the other side of the river and couldn't believe their eyes when the trees opened up to the sight of some Gen Zs splashing about on a shallow beach, he was glad that the river was now clean enough for swimming, or seemed to be.

It was hot, one of those steaming hot days that happens in Glasgow every so often. Old people complain about the stickiness in the air and after 3 or 4 days of heat people go crazy and gangs start stabbing rivals. Hot and humid and sweaty, clouds had been forming all day and he knew there would be a thunderstorm at some point. He had almost called off the walk because he was paranoid about being caught under trees when lightning flashed.

The path twisted and turned through the dense woods, the towering trees casting deep shadows that danced with the occasional beam of sunlight piercing through the canopy. The air was thick with the scent of damp earth and fallen leaves. As they walked, a strange hush seemed to fall over the group, the sounds of distant laughter and splashing from the river fading into the background.

Helena, who had been in high spirits just moments ago, now walked in silence, her eyes darting nervously towards the dense undergrowth on either side of the path. The black cat, which had briefly disappeared from sight, reappeared ahead of them, its yellow eyes glinting in the dim light. It moved with an unsettling grace, as if it knew the secrets hidden in the shadows.

"Do you think it's following us?" Helena whispered, her voice barely audible over the sound of their footsteps on the mossy ground.

"Nah, it's just a curious cat," he replied, though even as he said it, he felt a strange unease creeping into his thoughts. There was something about the way the cat moved, something almost deliberate, as if it were leading them somewhere.

They pressed on, the path becoming narrower and more overgrown. The trees seemed to close in around them, their gnarled branches reaching out like skeletal fingers. The air grew cooler, and the light dimmed further, until it felt as though they were walking through twilight.

"Are we sure we're going the right way?" one of the boys asked, his voice tinged with uncertainty.

"Holmwood House should be just ahead," he replied, though the confidence in his voice was starting to waver. The path had become unfamiliar, as if they had taken a wrong turn somewhere along the way.

They continued walking, but the sense of disorientation only grew. The woods seemed to twist and shift around them, the landmarks he remembered from his youth nowhere to be found. The wooden fence that had once run alongside the path was now long gone, replaced by a tangled mess of roots and brambles.

Suddenly, the black cat darted across their path, disappearing into the underbrush. Helena gasped, and the group came to a halt.

"Did you see that?" she asked, her voice trembling. "It looked like it was trying to show us something."

Before anyone could respond, a low rumble of thunder echoed through the trees, and the first drops of rain began to fall. The storm, that had been threatening all day, was finally upon them.

"We need to find shelter," he said, his voice urgent. "There's an old hut not far from here. We can wait out the storm there."

They hurried along the path, the rain now falling in heavy sheets, turning the ground beneath their feet into a slick, muddy mess. The trees swayed and creaked in the wind, and the air was filled with the sharp scent of ozone.

After what felt like an eternity, they finally spotted the shelter through the trees, its brick walls covered in moss and its broken wooden roof weathered and worn but still standing. They ran inside, grateful for the respite, the roof leaked in several places, and rainwater pooled in puddles on the old stone floor.

As they huddled together, trying to stay dry, he couldn't shake the feeling that they were being watched. The woods outside were dark and silent, the storm dampening sounds of the river.

Then, just as suddenly as it had begun, the rain stopped. The storm passed, leaving the air cool and fresh, with the scent of wet earth lingering in the breeze.

"Let's get moving," he said, eager to reach Holmwood House and put the strange events of the day behind them.

They left and continued along the path, the woods now eerily silent. The black cat was nowhere to be seen, and the oppressive atmosphere that had hung over them seemed to have lifted.

As they neared the edge of the woods, the trees began to thin out, and the path became more familiar. Relief washed over him as he recognized the winding road that led up to the house. The grand building finally came into view, its imposing facade standing tall against the darkening sky.

But as they approached, something caught his eye. A faint light flickered in one of the upper windows, and he felt a chill run down his spine. The house had not been lived in for years, it was a museum now. There was no reason for anyone to be inside at this time. Maybe it was a caretaker.

"Did you see that?" one of his boys asked, his voice barely above a whisper.

He nodded, his heart pounding in his chest. "Yes. Let's go and check it out."

The group hesitated, but curiosity got the better of them. They crossed the newly mown lawn and approached the front door, its grand woodwork showing its age. With a deep breath, he pushed it open, the hinges creaking in protest.

The inside of the house was dark, they stepped cautiously into the foyer, their footsteps echoing on the marble floor. The light they had seen from outside was gone, but a strange feeling of being watched persisted.

They moved deeper into the house, the shadows seeming to shift and move around them. The grand staircase loomed ahead, its banister covered in dust and cobwebs. The walls were lined with portraits, their eyes following them as they ascended the stairs.

At the top of the stairs, they found themselves in a long, narrow hallway. The floorboards creaked under their weight, and the air grew colder with each step. The feeling of unease had returned, stronger than ever.

As they reached the end of the hallway, they found a door slightly ajar. A faint light spilled out from within, casting eerie shadows on the walls.

He pushed the door open and stepped inside. The room was empty, save for a single chair in the centre. On the chair sat the black cat, its yellow eyes gleaming in the dim light.

Helena gasped, and he turned to see her staring at the wall, opposite the chair. There, on a enormous mirror, written in the condensation were the words: "Welcome Home."

A cold shiver ran down his spine as he realised what had been bothering him all along. The house, the cat, the strange feeling of being watched—it was all connected to his past, to the memories he had long buried.

"We need to leave," he said, his voice shaking. "Now."

They turned and fled the room, the feeling of dread growing with every step. The house seemed to come alive around them, the walls closing in, the shadows reaching out to grab them.

They burst out the front door and ran down the path, he hobbling along on, not stopping until they were back at the edge of the woods. The storm had returned, the rain falling in heavy sheets once more, but they didn't care. They ran until they could run no more, finally collapsing on the wet ground, gasping for breath.

When they looked back, Holmwood House was gone, swallowed by the darkness of the storm. The path ahead was clear, leading them back to the safety of the bridge.

Later as they sat in the Queens Park Café, waiting for their food to be ready in the Anarkali, opposite the pub, he noticed a man staring at him intently. Helena said suddenly, "I can't find our keys to the AirBnB, I must have dropped them in the house. You have to go back and get them."

The man got up, walked over, and crouched before him a wide grin on his face, what fresh hell is this? he thought. "Danny, long time no see, so good to see you after all these years, welcome home!".

Mini Cone by Ellie Ness

A mini orange traffic cone attached next
to the exhaust catches my attention
WHAT FUN!
Parked on a single yellow outside the
college is a riot of colour with a
personalised plate,
hub caps alternate between red and orange,
Manga decal with aggressive characters punching out, not
down!

Could a student afford this?
Unlikely, so
I start to think about the owner –
a woman in her thirties?
A Media lecturer perhaps, still down with the kids
parking, harking back to her degree
passing on her knowledge to recalcitrant teens
forced to rely on First Bus to

get back across the city –
not for them, the dog friendly café or the
Lane Committee,
now now.
They dare to dream
spark ignited by the woman
putting her key in the ignition
as yellow line restrictions start.

A Walk in the Park by Karmjit Badesha

At the end of each year that Mary attended Shawlands Academy, she stood in front of Dr Cummings' desk as he pulled out his fountain pen and neatly scribbled 'attentive, well behaved, 100% attendance' across her report cards.

In 1979, one day after her sixteenth birthday, she left school. Before she could even think about qualifications or what she might like to do next, her mum got her a job working nights in the Gateway on Victoria Road in Govanhill. Under buzzing and stuttering lights, she pushed her heavy trolley around each aisle, filling the dark shelves with colourful cans and packets. At the end of her shifts she would leave the store, tins clacking in her handbag, as Mr Johnson locked up, bottles clinking inside his jacket.

To occupy her weekends, her dad got her a job selling tickets at The Plaza Ballroom. Crammed into a small booth by the double doors, blinded by the dazzlingly bright lights and chandeliers around her, she scrambled to keep up with the endless rattle of coins that were thrown at her by excited couples, handsome and beautiful, eager to get into that music, forget their week and prove their love.

The rest of the time Mary spent in her bedroom. Crowded by the family collies Elvis and Priscilla, she tried to read, listen to the radio or stared out the window at the people walking in the park.

Come Fridays, her parents would collect her pay packets, taking their share of her wages for 'digs money' and some other stuff they said that 'only adults had to worry about'. Mary never found out for sure where that money went, but her parents took a larger share, when her mum started stuffing more white slips into the back of her bedroom drawer and the number of empty cans, left by her dad, made the black bin bags rattle.

A few years after hearing 'if anything happens again, the girl's here to look after us' whispered into the darkness of the house, she surprised her family by quietly announcing she had bought herself a flat in Govanhill. In response to how the 'bloody hell' she had managed to do that, she explained that the owner was a kind old man who had agreed that she could pay a deposit and then settle up the rest in instalments through his lawyers. That was the last conversation she had with the Allens and within a few months she had moved out, losing contact with her family altogether.

The one bedroom tenement flat on Allison Street was sold by Mr McCulloch who had just retired and was planning to emigrate to stay with his daughter and grandchildren in Canada. The day she moved in was the day he was to fly out.

'Miss Allen, the keys to your new flat.'

He dropped them onto her palm then struggled down the stairs, banging the edge of his luggage trunk against the close walls and muttering that he wished that the Asians, who had just opened the curry house downstairs, had done so earlier. He loved their spicy food and the way the smell lifted up to his windows. Closing her door gently, Mary turned the latch on each lock and then sat stretched out on her new sofa. Wrapped in silence, she wiggled her toes as she picked another slice of pineapple rings out of the tin, the syrupy juice overflowing and dripping onto the towel on her lap.

Mary got her first dog Stanley, a small white and caramel spotted Jack Russell with a quiet yap, later that year. At ten o'clock she would slip on her walking shoes and long coat to take Stanley for a walk up to Victoria Road. Stride for stride they walked together, the leash loose in her hand.

From there, they would turn left and the two of them would walk past Singh's Hardware saying 'Hello' to the tall owner with the thick beard and turban, who would be fighting to balance all of his ladders outside his store. Stanley would slow down outside Auld's bakery as Sandra and Margaret set out a fresh batch of sausage pies and pause to match sniffs with Gordon's golden retriever Frankie, who was tied up outside the Queen's Park Cafe.

At the top of Victoria Road they would enter through the tall black gates of Queen's Park and do a circuit under tall trees, past the Victoria Infirmary and then around the duck and boating pond, where Stanley would pad cautiously around the water's edge, amazed and suspicious of the elegant swans.

Those walks lasted longer when Stanley started to develop arthritis in his back legs, when he turned twelve. Skipping with a limp that caused his ears to flap like birds' wings, they followed the same path across Govanhill and were back in time for lunch and the last bit of the news. Until the day Mary came home walking fast along Victoria Road, the lead empty and scraping along the ground.

She waited a respectful time to adopt Charles, a happy white West Highland Terrier. He quickly became a celebrity in the area, who needed to stop by everyone he passed, so he could get a smell of their hands and then agree to a stroke. Maybe that was the reason he ran up and down the hall, a full half hour before they left, then started to paw at the door, while Ms Mary Allen put on her trainers and took down her waterproof jacket from the peg, next to Stanley's old collar and lead.

He had finished scratching off the second coat of paint Mary had put on the door and was happily working on the third, when on a walk up to the Flagpole, he was attacked by a runaway Rottweiler. From then on, Charles hid and whimpered before each walk and whined miserably when anyone approached him.

When Mary locked up for the night, Charles would dash down the hall and jump onto her bed, asleep by the time she checked the doors were locked and all the lights switched off. Sleeping around him bent at an angle, her back was stiff and ached in the mornings.

When Charles passed away suddenly of heart failure fifteen years later, Mary waited another few months before she bought Max, a cheerful wee mix of a dog that had a drooping tongue that never seemed to fit into his smiling mouth. The puppy learned quickly to keep in check with her shuffling steps and walking stick. Max resisted all doggy temptations and stuck close to Mary, staring up at her with his wide bright eyes.

Mary walked her dogs around Govanhill every day. During the big storm in 1987, Stanley delighted in the riches of branches knocked down to the ground, while she walked carefully around the toppled trees caught by the park fencing, crushing them into bent and distorted fingers.

She cut through the protests outside the Govanhill Baths in 2001, when it seemed the whole community came out and shouted that they wanted the council to rethink its decision. Charles barked cheerfully with the drums, catching the attention of someone who yelled even the 'dug knows that closing the baths down is a crazy idea'. His photo was pictured in that month's issue of the Glaswegian newspaper, Mary standing puzzled beside him.

She didn't go into the park for days after that 'poor girl' was killed inside, long after the police and reporters left, and the last of the thin fluttering blue and white tape lay trampled in the mud.

She walked unsteadily through the foot high snow in 2010, carrying Max when he sank in up to his belly. She passed Mr Singh as he barked orders from his wheelchair, instructing his son to put down more gravel and at the same time he wanted him to get more sledges from the van. Up on the slopes of the park, a jagged chorus of delighted fright followed the careening paths of those sledges, cutting through the snow until there were only long muddy trails behind them.

The next few days Mary and Max walked carefully through the dirty red slushy path, shovelled out on the pavement. She had to put her boots on the radiator for a week to dry them out and Max growled his unhappiness, as she sprayed him down in the bath.

Mary gripped the traffic lights, when the last of the rumbling Gateway trucks cleared out the store and the first of the Somerfield delivery trucks came in. By the time those trucks were replaced with banners for Lidl, it no longer mattered or worried her. The sparkle and allure of The Plaza had fizzled out long ago, finally extinguished by the swinging wrecking ball that cut in, accompanied by an orchestra of construction work that flirted around new luxury apartments.

She only missed three days of walks during the entirety of the Covid Pandemic. Shaking her head at the worsening news reports, she tucked her white hair behind the strings of her mask before she left her flat. Standing outside the shuttered shop fronts of Oxfam, Ramsay's and the Anarkali, Mary and Max stared at their reflections. Hastily drawn up signs covered opening times and menus, explaining to the empty world that they would be closed for a bit but were looking forward to seeing their customers soon.

Safely through the pandemic with little more than a niggling cough, Mary noticed that Max was not his usual self. After another week of leaving more of his evening dinners, she took him to the vets and they confirmed the worst, finding a lump on his belly. Stroking his tired head on the examination table, they told her to prepare herself, that his condition would deteriorate and she would need to consider taking action to prevent him suffering.

Max clearly ignored the vet's assessment. He rallied back to his usual self but then passed away in December 2023, a full 8 months after that diagnosis. He had gone to bed one night after finishing off a full can of dog food and then some rich tea biscuits. He snuggled up in his basket by her bed and when she woke up in the morning, he did not jump up to get his morning stroke. She found him still sleeping in his bed, cold but smiling, with some small crumbs on his beard.

Mary is standing on her doormat, holding her mop and watching as the wet landing begins to dry into patches of clean grey. Her neighbours, the Rahelas, join her on the landing, ready to take Alina to her first day at primary school. The young girl is wrapped up tight in her new uniform and jacket. Mary comments on how big she is getting, that she will soon make lots of friends in school, and that it's very important she be a good girl for her teacher.

Alina beams a big smile as her backpack slides down again, catching in her elbows and hitting the back of her legs. Her parents ask when Mrs Allen will be getting herself a new dog. Alina misses Max a lot. Mary smiles softly as she squeezes the mop dry in the bucket and says that she is going to get a cat soon, maybe two, she really did not like all the walking involved with having a dog.

The Sou'side Settler by Shirley Mackie

There once was a lass fae the East
Auld Reekie's streets to say not the least
Every inch o this toon she did ken
Fae it's dreich cowgate tae the hills & the Glen

Twenty years there oor lass did bide
The cobbled streets filled their bairn wi' pride
She loved her hame wi' aw her heart
Ne'er did she dream they e'er would part

But fate had a different plan
When oor lass did meet a Glesga man
She ventured through tae the Wild West
Wi' warnings a plenty that the Weeg wisnae the best

For a new adventure she wiz fair ready
So she boarded that bus wi' a hand o so steady
Nae place allowed for nerves or fear
Mind the safety o hame wiz ay sae near

Upon descending the City Link
Oor girl's heart surely failed to sink
Sometimes love can be an instant thing
A full heart did indeed this city bring

The Glesga man she had travelled tae see
No up tae much, no her cup o tea
But this fair city sure melted her heart
And a move tae Glasgow was tae be her final part

But where in the city would she call hame
Time tae explore, where would she tame
The West End she decided tae settle
Her fellow students were in fine fettle

A year stayed she aff the Byer's road
Happy hours n boozy brunches in overload
Fair knackered, fate decided tae play her hand
When one day a daunder doon the sou'side wiz tae be had

She had ne'er before ventured South
Aghasp & agawk did she find her mouth
What stunning place wiz this
The folks, the streets, the parks, aww bliss

Amongst these streets she had tae be
Awa fae fellow students she'd feel free
So quickly the move was tae be made
And new roots were soon tae be laid

Here she met the real folk
No West End accent wiz to be spoke
Welcomed wiz she wi' open arms
Sou'siders keen tae share their charms

A year in Shawlands she did enjoy
The pub next door most keen to employ
A pal a plenty she did meet
Aww the punters she was happy to greet

In The hustle & bustle o' Shawlands cross
She found fair comfort ne'er dross
The busy streets were fu o life
The sounds o laughter were oh so rife

But we Cannae live wi' constant voice

At times we need a break fae the noise
A tranquil place was soon to be found
Amongst the leaves a mair peaceful sound

Queens Park became her place o refuge
Many a stroll, ignoring the deluge
To wander idly for hours & hours
Losing yersel' amongst the foliage n flowers

What a braw wee way to pass the time
Ignoring the bells that threatened tae chime
Wi' a book an a bench an a coffee in tow
Ne'er a rush, naewhere needed tae go

The gentler sound o birds singin' away
Brightened the skies on the dreichest o day
The cries o the weans playin oan the swing
A warmth tae the heart an smile they did bring

Then a daunder up the Vicky Road
Saw oor lass up sticks n heave her load
Seven years she bided up there
Wi' memories a plenty an stories tae share

The culinary meltin pot she did embrace
Desperate tae try every new taste
Cultures a plenty found round these parts
Wi' everyone together in Glasgow's big heart

Desire for a move wan mair time
But tae leave the Sou'side would be but a crime
Time tae gie up busy Tenement life
O'er to the Shields where the Avenues are rife

A proper muckle hoose wi' a garden n aw
Nae noisy neighbours tae be found was sae braw

A stones throw fae aw the delights of afore
But plenty new places for me tae explore

A wee park just a hunner yards fae the door
Wildlife a plenty an dugs galore
Wi' Pollok just right roon' the corner
Spoilt for choice for a Sou'side jaunter

Near thirty yon year since deciding tae stay
Seems like fate did indeed get her way
Many a change hae been witnessed throughout
The Sou'side could ne'er I be without

Grown older an wiser with these leafy streets
The stories we share would be gie hard tae beat
My bairns brought up here amongst Sou'side kin
Thegither they played roon the streets, what a din

Tales o' the past I love them tae hear
Like the auld Queen who ran fae the battle in fear
Tae watch them explore the parks I once found
The places my heart will forever be bound

Plenty a story still tae be made
In this fabulous place so much mair to be said
It's an honour tae call the Sou'side my hame
A return tae Auld Reekie wid ne'er be but the same

A celebration o humanity is here tae be found
The Sou'side voice is loud and fair proud.

Finding Blackie McGinlay by Lesley O'Brien

'Malky, Malky, have ye seen Blackie, have ye seen him? Ah left him here. Tied up aboot 10 minutes ago and noo he's vanished!'

'Whit de ye mean vanished?', asked Malky as he scraped impatiently at the cellophane wrapper of ten Benson and Hedges cigarettes. Malky was Thomas' younger cousin, he lived on Main Street Bridgeton, in the tenement close, next to the One-O-One Off Sales.

'Ah wis jist in the Oaffy fur ma da's wee quarter boatle, he always sends me on a Monday when he gets his pension. Ah tied Blackie tae the pole right there and noo he's no' there!'

Thomas began to beat his right hand against his chest, something he'd done since he was a boy when stressed.

'Look, ye better calm doon, Thomas, he'll no' be far. Have ye goat yer inhaler wae ye? Yer soundin' breathless, son. Ye better take a wee puff.'

Thomas was frantically marching from the corner of Main Street and Dalmarnock Road, towards the taxi rank at the other side of Bridgeton Cross. He didn't hear Malky's concern, his mind was buzzing and his heart was full of fear of what his dad might do, when he heard he had lost his beloved wee dog, Blackie McGinlay. His dad always gave the dog its full name. Thomas imagined he'd had him baptised at the chapel. He believed his dad loved that dog more than him. He crossed the road looking straight ahead, luckily there was no traffic coming. Usually, he paused cautiously at the edge of the kerb, hearing his mother's voice in his head, 'Mind, Thomas, you stop, look and listen before crossin' that busy road.' Right now he could only think of one thing and that was finding Blackie McGinlay.

'Hey, you. Get tae the end o' the queue, whit dae ye think yer daein, skipping in, in front o' everybody?'

'Aw mister I need tae find my da's wee dug, have ye seen it? A wee black pit bull terrier, aboot this height?' Thomas bent over and put his hand just below his duffle coat and looked up, hopefully to the man at the front of the queue. 'He's dead friendly, he'd lick ye tae death, he'd never bite ye.'

'Look pal, I'm gonna fuckin bite ye if ye don't get tae the end o' the queue!'

'Thomas, Thomas, come 'ere.' Halfway down the queue was Johnny, Thomas' next-door neighbour. Johnny was the only son of Mr and Mrs McIver. The McIvers lived on the first floor of a tenement flat at 30 Dalmarnock Road, above Mitchells the Funeral Directors. Their door faced the flat of the McGinlays, where Thomas lived with his dad. Johnny McIver was twenty-two years old; half of Thomas' age and a considerable part of those years had been spent tormenting Thomas. Thomas' mother, Mary had died at seventy-four of a heart attack. Her pregnancy with Thomas had left her with angina. She'd often worried what would happen to her youngest son, Thomas, when she passed.

Thomas heard his mother's voice again in his head, 'You jist keep away fae that Johnny McIver, he's a bad yin, he'll come tae a sticky end. Ye hear me Thomas, keep away fae Johnny McIver.'

'Have ye loast Blackie? Oh yer da'll be furious Thomas. Whit ye gonna dae? Ye cannae go hame without 'im.'

'I'm jist gonna get a taxi to take me tae the fitba' pitches, at the Green. That's ees favourite place. Ah cannae walk that far the day, cos ma asthma's playin' up, and ye know I've only got eight toes, cos ae ma accident when ah was wee. I've goat ma birthday money in ma pocket. It wis ma birthday yesterday, so I'll be able to pay fur a taxi. I goat a rubik cube an aw for ma birthday, but that's in the hoose. So, wull ye let me go in front o' ye in the queue, Johnny?'

'Look, I've goat a better idea, Thomas. We could share a taxi. I need to drap somethin' aff tae a pal in the Gorbals. We could keep an eye oot fur Blackie on the way.'

'Aye, awright then, that's a good idea.' Thomas took his place in the queue beside Johnny. 'I hope ah find em soon, it's pure freezin the night. Look, ah can even see ma breath, it's that cauld.' The cold air caught the back of his throat and he suddenly began to wheeze and gasp for breath.

'Blackie'll be fine, he's goat 'is ain fur coat remember. Anyway, never mind that, there's oor taxi.'

Thomas squeezed slowly into the back of the black cab. He was 6 feet 1 and the cold December night gnawed at the arthritis in his left hip. He reached into the inside pocket of his coat, amidst the sticky pile of Blackjack sweetie papers was the familiar shape of his wooden box that contained his glass asthma inhaler. Thomas opened it carefully, unfolded the cotton handkerchief that held it in place, put the mouthpiece to his lips and quickly took two sharp blasts of his medication.

'Ocht, don't look sae worried Thomas. We'll find yer da's wee dug. Hutchie flats in the Gorbals, driver and can you go up James Street, slowly, we're lookin for a wee dug.'

'Aye, nae bother pal. Whit kinda dug is it yiv lost?'

Thomas peered intently out of the window, his left hand grasped the handle above the door, his body tense and his breathing laboured.

'It's a black pit bull terrier driver, apparently it'll lick ye tae death', said Johnny, as he poked Thomas, playfully in the ribs.

'Right. I'll put a call oot on the radio and we'll have aw the taxi drivers in Glesga oan the lookout for wee…whit's its name?'

'It's Blackie, his name's Blackie McGinlay', replied Thomas. For the first time since he got into the taxi, Thomas took his eyes off the road. 'Is Blackie gonnae be oan the radio? Can ye ask them tae play ma favourite tune. It's Waterloo, by…em, whit's their name again? Ah stayed up late, watchin them oan the telly. They won the Eurovision song contest. Did ye see it?'

'Naw, ya eejit, it's no Radio fucking Clyde, he's talkin aboot, it's the taxi radio! He's gonna ask aw the ither taxi drivers tae look oot for wee Blackie.'

'Aw, right!'

Thomas nodded but he wasn't sure what Johnny meant. He'd been in a taxi twice before, once to his grandpa's funeral and the other to Buchanan Street bus station, when he went on holiday to Blackpool with his mum and dad. He peered out the window, desperately hoping to see the familiar wag of Blackie's tail.

'Can ye slow doon a bit driver, this is Blackie's favourite bit', said Thomas, as he slid forward onto the edge of his seat.

'Aye, nae bother son.'

Thomas, Johnny, and the taxi driver scanned the pavement outside, that skirted the edges of Glasgow Green on both sides of the road. The park was cloaked in darkness, they could just make out the white outline of goalposts from the football pitches and the silhouette of a woman walking her dog. As she passed under the orange glow of the streetlight, their eyes were drawn to the excitable tail of a Border Collie puppy. It was pulling hard on the end of its lead, dragging the woman with a sudden jolt over to the lamppost.

'Aww that looks jist like Lassie. It's goat the exact same coat as Lassie, well ah think it's the same, white and kinda Irn Bru colour. Ah cannae tell on oor black and white telly. Ah love watchin' Lassie, ah watch it every Saturday mornin.' The frown on Thomas's face was briefly replaced with a smile.

'Aye, well, looks like Lassie's taking her owner fur a walk, a wee live wire, that yin', the taxi driver smirked as he slowly took the bend in the road and switched on his full beams. The Glasgow Green flashed from darkness to full colour. Silver birch, rowan and oak trees with coats of emerald green moss and golden lichen appeared like the flick of a page from a book of fairy tales.

'Nae sign o' your wee dug then, son?'

'Naw. No' yet. Ma daddy's gonna kill me. He pure loves that dug.'

'Right, ah know!', said Johnny. 'I'll ask ma pals in the Gorbals tae be oan the lookoot fur Blackie. Driver can ye take us noo tae the Hutchie flats?'

Johnny took a packet of Golden Virginia tobacco from the chest pocket of his denim jacket. Sitting back in his seat, he sprinkled some of the tobacco leaf into a cigarette paper and with an expert flick, rolled himself a cigarette. He stretched over and opened the window at his side.

'Aww that cigarette is pure stinkin.' Thomas screwed up his face, as Johnny lit the cigarette and smoke filled the back of the cab.

'It's no' the ciggy yer smellin, it's the stink o' the malt fae the distillery.'

Johnny pointed to Strathclyde Whisky Distillery on the other side of Ballater street. It sat on the south bank of the River Clyde, its single silver chimney reached 200 feet into the night sky. Amidst giant puffs of grey-white steam, the distillery appeared like an old paddle steamer, sailing 'doon the watter.'

As blue smoke from Johnny's cigarette was sucked out of the window, the bitter smell of tobacco was replaced with the thick malty stench of fermenting barley.

'Aww don't ye jist love it?' Johnny put his head out of the window and took a deep breath. 'Cannae let the angels keep it aw fur themselves.'

'Angels?' Thomas looked at Johnny, suspiciously. 'You're trying tae wind me up. There's no' any angels oot there.'

'Nawww, ahm no! It's a thing people say, the *angels share*, it's the whisky that goes up intae the air.'

'So angels drink whisky?' Thomas was sure Johnny was at his old tricks, trying to make a fool of him.

'Naw! Well, aye...ocht never mind!'

'He's right son', the taxi driver pitched in, 'It's just a saying, *the angels share,* jist a wee story, folks imagine the angels drinkin' the whisky that evaporates when it's maturin.'

'Aww right! Ah never goat *that* story at Sunday school.'

The taxi driver laughed, 'Pity they don't tell that yin at Sunday School. They might get mair punters if they told stories like that.' Thomas could see the driver's shoulders shaking as his hands held firmly to the wheel.

Every Sunday morning, Thomas attended the eleven o'clock mass at Sacred Heart Chapel on Reid Street, a handsome red sandstone building that sat aside Sacred Heart primary school, a modern monstrosity of 1970's brutalist architecture. Granny Moffat, his mother's mother, had been a protestant, a follower of Glasgow Rangers and member of the Orange Lodge. A framed print of King William of Orange on his horse, proudly on her bedroom wall, facing a faded sepia tinted photo of her mother. Granny Moffat had sent Thomas, from the age of six to twelve years old, to the Evangelical Presbyterian, Bethany Hall Sunday School. Thomas often sang the hymns he'd learned there, as he made his way out of his flat and down the stairs of his tenement close. He loved to hear his voice boom against the old stone walls.

'Kin ye stoap here please driver, where that van's parked in front ae the flats. Jist wait here fur me Thomas. Ah'll no be a minute.'

Johnny got out of the taxi and approached a young man in double denim who appeared from behind a pale blue Bedford van. Thomas looked out of the taxi window and craned his neck, trying to see the rooftop of the Queen Elizabeth flats. The residents had named the three blocks, Barlinnie, Alcatraz and Singsong. Twenty stories of grey concrete riddled with dampness and asbestos. He began to count the floors by counting the windows from the bottom to the top. He'd been to the flats with his mother when he was a teenager to visit her old work pal from Woolworths. They had sent him to the shop for milk, but Thomas got lost on the way back. He couldn't remember which floor, or which block she lived on. The memory slowly came back to him as he counted, accompanied with a crushing feeling of dread.

'Are ye awright there, son? Yer looking awfy worried. I'll check in wae the controller, see if any o' the other drivers have seen yer wee dug.'

Thomas felt his stomach somersault, as he remembered why he was in the taxi.

'Blackie'll be pure starvin by noo. Ma da usually geez em the other half ae a tin o' dug food at this time.'

Thomas put his hands in his pockets looking for a sweetie. 'Aw naw and I've still goat ma Da's whisky! Ah forgoat aw aboot that!'

Thomas could feel his chest tighten.

'Ah need some fresh air.'

Frantically grabbing at the door of the taxi, he swung it open and walked over to the back of the van. He leaned against its back door and tried to remember the breathing exercises the school nurse had taught him. Thomas counted as he inhaled but his mind was distracted as he became aware of a strange but familiar smell wafting from his left side.

'Aye it's the best o' gear, Wullie, rolled by the virgins o' the Himalayas and geez ye a lovely wee stone. Everybody's efter a bit. An ye'll no get it any cheaper. Hear, try it, ye'll see whit a mean.'

Thomas forgot about his breathing exercises, as he tuned into Wullie and Johnny's conversation. He remembered what the strange smell was and peeked his head around the end of the van, just in time to see Johnny pass Wullie a small rectangular package, wrapped in newspaper. Wullie sniffed at the package then took a long hard drag on the roll-up in his other hand.

'Ah man, that's nice…mmm… tastes and smells fucking brilliant.' Wullie handed Johnny a thick wad of cash.

Thomas suddenly felt something touch his shoes. It was a small black pit bull terrier, sniffing intently.

'Blackie, Blackie, where have ye been? Aw thank God I found ye!' Thomas patted the dog on the head as it jumped excitedly and licked his hands.

'Who the fuck are you?' Wullie puffed out his chest and took a few steps towards Thomas. 'Hey you, whit ye daen wae ma dug?'

'Calm doon, Wullie, it's aw right, its ma neighbour Thomas. He's hairmless, tuppence aff the shillin', but he's awright. He's loast 'is dug, he thinks your Kim is his wee Blackie.'

'Aww naw! Is that no' Blackie, is that yir dug? I thought it wis Blackie, he looks dead like him, bit skinnier though.' Thomas clapped the pit bull terrier that was now sniffing eagerly around the edges of his duffel coat.

'Nae wonder he looks like Blackie, yer Da bought Blackie aff o' Wullie. Kim here is Blackie's wee brother', said Johnny, pointing at the dog.

'No way! I think he can smell Blackie aff ma coat.' Kim was jumping onto Thomas's shins.

The conversation was suddenly interrupted by the sound of the taxi door slamming shut.

'Aye, it's a cauld yin the night, boys. Here son, is that yer wee dug? Have ye found em?' The taxi driver zipped up his black leather bomber jacket as he walked towards the three men and the dog.

'Naw, it's no' him, it's ees wee brother', said Thomas shaking his head, his voice tense with anxiety and heavy with disappointment.

'Ah right, well then, ah think I've goat some bad news fur ye son. Wan o' the other drivers has just seen a wee dug, that fits Blackie's description, being run oe'r wae a number 46 bus on the Saltmarket. I'm afraid he's a gonner, son.'

'Aw naw, naaaaaaaaaaaaw! No wee Blackie! Naw. Naaaaaw! Ah cannae go hame. Ma Da'll pure kill me.' Tears were pouring down Thomas's cheeks.

'Look, it's awright Thomas, calm doon.' As Johnny put his hand on Thomas's back, he could feel his body shake and gasp for breath.

'Take a few puffs o' yer inhaler Thomas, ye'll be awright son.' Johnny put his hand into Thomas's inside coat pocket and placed the box with his inhaler into the palm of Thomas's hand. 'Here take a few puffs on that, ye'll feel better in a wee minute.'

Thomas sucked hard on the mouthpiece of his inhaler and squeezed on the rubber ball attached to the bottle. As the vapor hit the back of his throat, he coughed, his chest was tight and wheezing like the high-pitched whistle of an old steam train.

'Right Thomas, look, I've goat an idea. Wullie wis jist sayin he's sick a walkin' the dug at night. Why don't ye buy Kim aff Wullie and yer Da'll never know the difference. You've still goat yer birthday money, hint ye?', said Johnny as he leaned over and whispered in Thomas's ear. 'And ah can keep a secret if you kin. You know whit ah mean, Thomas. Ah know ye clocked whit happened there wae me and Wullie. And I know you've tried the auld wacky backy yersel, cos it wis me that gied ye it! Mind ye were sic as a parrot. Ah hid tae cairt ye up the stairs and yer mammy pit ye tae bed. So best we aw keep shtoom aboot the night and anyway', said Johnny, as he looked over at Wullie, 'yer Da'll never notice the difference between Blackie and 'is wee brother here. Right, Wullie?'

'Aye, bit the thing is Johnny', said Wullie, shaking his head, 'Blackie's wee brother is actually Blackie's wee sister. Kim's a bitch, no a stud!'

Johnny winked at Wullie. 'That disnae matter, auld McGinlay'll no' even notice. Look, Thomas don't worry. C'mon we'll go and get Blackie. We'll gie em a nice wee send aff. We'll bury him doon at his favourite bit at the fitba' pitches. Bit mind, no' a word tae yer Da or tae anybody else aboot whit happened the night. So, the story is, Blackie went missin', ah helped ye find im and we aw lived happily ever efter. Right, Thomas?'

Battlefield - a tableaux by Boris Pichotka

Battlefield, a name at once thrilling and foreboding. "It's where Mary Stuart mustered her army for the final battle on Scottish Soil," the plaque on Battlefield Road tells me.

Today, nothing could be further from that historical reality. I pass the time, waiting for the number five bus, a Matcha Latte in my hand.

It is early spring and behind me, the hulking silhouette of the new housing development that has taken over what only ten years ago was still a working hospital, obscures any view of the daffodils in the park. This new development with its sand-coloured brick and coppery cladding has been controversial, yet the people of Battlefield are a far cry from the historic army that assembled here in 1568.

Today's locals are keyboard warriors, trading gossip like insults and whose vorpal blades are often blunted by grammatical lapses they bear as badges of honour. One minute their focus is on the acute shortage of parking, that is sure to bring everything to its knees, the next the seemingly ever changing opening hours of local brunch spots and cafes draw their ire.

When the schools are on holiday, a quiet descends over the area that is hard to describe. If our weather were hotter, one might almost think the area between Battlefield Road and the White Cart is having a midday siesta. Things feel sleepy. A solitary car goes down Ledard Road, past the telephone exchange and turns into Lochleven Drive - new tyres from Motor Sound. On Cartside Street, a big ginger tom stretches lazily in the sun, the tip of his tail flicking up every so often as he ignores the keening of the seagulls circling above. In the distance, across the river, the rhythmic *plock-plo-plock* of tennis balls or maybe the *thwack* of a cricket bat as it hits the ball to the delight of the small crowd of spectators.

Once, I think it was the summer of the first lockdown, a man floated down the White Cart, holding a can of beer aloft from his inflatable. It had been a hot day, too hot for seeing otters. Did he spot the heron, wading in the shallows, as he drifted past? Did he look up to see the bats hanging from the underside of the bridge at Tantallon Road? Who was he and where had he come from? Had he ridden his rubber ring down the rapids at Snuff Mill Bridge?

When Halloween comes with the scent of autumn leaves, pumpkin spice lattes and cinnamon swirls, the streets are wet and black. It's a cold, dreich night, and October storms rattle the sash windows. I set to work, carving my Jack-o'-lantern and plan the design for the Winter Wanderland, when the band strikes up: "Ghost Town" by the Specials. It's a motley crew who follow the marching brass: young and old, their paper lanterns swinging desperately in the wind, their little lights battling the darkness. From my window I watch them go by: skeletons and witches, little dinosaurs and pirates.

In mid-December rare snow covers the area. A white blanket that muffles all sounds except the crunching of boots. Two men and their dog head up the hill as in the pitch black, all in winter coats wrapped up against the cold. Their destination? The Christmas tree lot behind National Tyres. They have just bought their first flat and this will be their first real Christmas tree. The chosen Norseman is a big beast, two metres tall and wider than ideal, but it was chosen with their Frenchie's approval. With practised ease, the shorter of the two hoists the massive tree onto his shoulder, his fingers grabbing a branch through the netting. Slip-sliding, they make it back down the hill and into the close. Soon the lights twinkle, candy canes, wooden ornaments and dried slices of fruit adorn the tree, silver and gold bells add sparkle and at the top, a star in red gingham. It fills most of the bay window. It's big, slightly crooked and by no means perfect, but it's theirs and it's home.

MOTHER'S BLESSINGS by Elizabeth R. Etheridge

She hung the last of the washing on the fraying rope, lifted the wet clothes with her left hand, the pole with her right, and pushed them out the first-floor tenement window until the pole rested in the anchor stop on the well-worn kitchen window ledge. It had been a long day and it was still only half-two. Most Saturdays she would be off up the Paisley Road for the week's messages, but he didn't come home last night with his brew money so she knew it was odds on he'd blown the lot.

Old Molly came in with some chips and a bottle of ginger for the weans. When they'd demolished their chips, she gave them a penny each for the Saturday matinee at the pictures. The weans happily scrambled down the stairs and off to the cinema on Cornwall St.

Molly lived directly across the street from Margaret in the close next to the police office. And though a fine-looking woman in her time, she'd never married. It was rumored her fiancé had been killed in the war.

"Margaret, are you alright hen?" asked Molly as she watched the weans happily skipping up the street.

Margaret burst into tears. "I'm just so tired. I don't know how I'm gonnae manage Molly. I've nae money for the factor, or tae get the light put back on. And see, look, there in last night's Times, that's oor address! A Sheriff's Sale for oor hoose next Thursday! Whit am I tae dae Molly? There's nothing left tae sell!"

Molly, all of four feet nothing, took Margaret by the shoulders, marched her back to the kitchen, and sat her down in the chair in front of the waning fire. "I'll make us a wee cuppa tea Margaret." Humming to herself, she filled the teapot at the sink and lit the gas burner. Molly never knew what to say in these situations, but she always knew what to do. When the teapot boiled, she threw in the last half-teaspoon of loose-leaf tea from the black and gold tea-caddy on top of the gas cooker. Getting two cups from the press, she was just about to pour the tea when there came a heavy pounding on the door.

"Oh my god! It's the Polis!" whispered Margaret. "Don't open it Molly. Don't open it."

The pounding increased. "Police! Open up!"

Margaret crossed herself in prayer as she went to the lobby and opened the door. Standing there were two policemen and between them hung Frank, her man, legless drunk.

"Are you going to take him in?" asked the sergeant.

"Where'd you find him?" said Margaret.

"He was lying in the pen beside Munros the butcher. Seems he's lost a fight."

"What are you talking about?" asked Margaret.

The two officers hauled Frank up and pulled his head back. His face was covered in dried blood.

"Oh my god, bring him in! Put him on the bed!"

The two men dragged the semi-conscious Frank in and threw him on the recess bed tucked into the wall of the small kitchen. "We'll be off now." said the sergeant.

"And good riddance tae bad rubbish," said Molly as she closed the door behind them. "That sergeant is a right bad yin," she said helping Margaret slip the shoes off Frank.

Pulling off his jacket and trousers, Margaret raked through the pockets. "Worthless bastard! There's no' a penny left. But oh aye, he's got his tobacco tin filled. And look at aw these betting slips!" Throwing the lot at the unconscious Frank she burst into tears and cried, "Whit am I tae dae?"

Molly went back to the teapot and began pouring the tea. "You know what Margaret, you and the weans should come over to mine's and stay the night. There's plenty of room and there's plenty to eat."

"Oh no, I couldn't put you to aw that trouble Molly," replied Margaret.

Molly had offered help many times before, but Margaret, always embarrassed, refused.

"It'll teach that miserable lump a lesson," insisted Molly. "When he wakes up the night to no electricity and no family, it'll give him a right fright! Aye, that would serve him right."

Two by two the weans splashed and played in Molly's big bathtub. Bath time for Margaret's weans was usually the rusted tin bath in front of the kitchen fire. By the time the eldest got in, the water was manky and cold. Molly made some beans on toast, while Margaret dried and dressed the weans for bed. The weans, oblivious to the reason for the sleepover, happily shared what happened with the cowboys at the pictures in between shovels of beans and toast. By nine o'clock they were all sound asleep in Molly's big double bed.

"Away and take yourself a nice long bath Margaret," said Molly. "I'll clean this up."

"Oh that would be lovely Molly, are ye sure?"

"Aye, away you go lassie, there's some nice lavender bath salts in the lobby press. Help yourself hen."

Margaret couldn't remember the last time she'd had a real bath. What with two part-time jobs, taking care of the weans, the house, and her drunk of a man, there was never enough time for baths. Her bath was a quick wash at the kitchen sink before the weans were up. The lavender scent, soothed her weary soul and sent her drifting off.

"Margaret hen, are you all right in there? You've no' done yourself in, have you?" asked Molly tapping on the door.

Startled Margaret awoke. "Aye, I'm fine Molly, I just drifted aff."

In the kitchen she found a digestive biscuit and a glass of warm milk sitting on the table. "Aw, thanks Molly. My Mammy used to aye make us a glass o' warm milk at bedtime. God, I miss her." With both hands around the glass, her head dropped and tears trickled down her face.

"Och, come oan now lassie, it'll be alright. Away and get a good night's sleep. The morra's another day and who knows what blessings that'll bring."

As Margaret climbed into the big double bed with her six sleeping weans, they shifted and cooried into her. "I'm blessed right enough Molly." she whispered tucking the blankets around them.

"Aye hen, you really are. Night night."

Getting fit by Marco Giannasi

It was a miserable winter night in February 2019 when I realised I was actually getting old and approaching 65. I desperately grabbed my iPad and searched online for a magic way to feel young again: Vitamins! Treatments! Plastic Surgery! Then I realised this was not the right path to take. Only after browsing alternative ways to get fit and reading about Kuk Sool Won did it all come together, and it appeared my quest was answered!

I decided to give this traditional Korean martial arts system a try and contacted the local Kuk Sool Won Club. I asked the organiser, Andrew, if it was ok for, shall we say, a mature man to enrol. His answer was very clear: "YES, there are no age limits." So, I decided to have a go.

One Wednesday night, very nervous and with second thoughts, my wife, Yellena, drove me to the door of the Club. I hesitated to step out of the car, however Yellena was not taking NO for an answer and basically pushed me out the car towards the club. Andrew was at the door and read my concerns. He reassured me I would be "fine" and with the right mental and physical attitude Kuk Sool Won would change my life around!

Right away I encountered my first challenge which was to climb three flights of stairs – 84 steps in total – while trying to keep up a casual conversation with Andrew and trying not to appear out of breath. As we both walked in, I saw a group of very fit and alarmingly young-looking guys which sapped my confidence and confirmed me in my belief that I was going beyond my comfort zone in terms of my fitness and ability.

However, I had committed to a full 3 hours' class including acrobatics that was more like Cirque du Soleil. To my immense surprise and delight I survived the experience. Though at the end of the session I was exhausted, I felt excited and ALIVE and realised that I had the ability to seriously improve my life and wellbeing.

At the end of the class as I made my way out and was about to go downstairs, panic seized me as I fleetingly lost control over my legs, and I looked like I was trying to impersonate ROBO COP! Wow, that was an alarm bell ringing telling me how unfit and weak I had become.

Would I dare go back???

Lies by Iain Bain

I have long been envious of my wife's talent in being able to raise one eyebrow. I have once or twice practised in the mirror but never mastered my own woolly and wayward brow, in the way that she has, in displaying dubiety or surprise. When she handed me the cream-coloured envelope, I suspect she knew fine well this would irk me, but for me to receive a formal letter in an unfamiliar hand, in this digital age, was bound to provoke her curiosity. It was an invitation to an evening in celebration of the retirement of one of my old teachers. There would be wine, finger food, whatever that meant, and a string quartet. It was more than surprising to me that I had been singled out to be asked to the event. There were generations of former pupils in his long career to choose from, some of whom had been successful, or at least well-known in their various lives and careers, including a couple of local politicians, a plumbing magnate and a singer in a heavy metal band. I was not one of them. Perhaps the organisers had mistaken me for someone else, with a similar name, or perhaps they were picking out names at random.

'Do you remember him?' my wife asked.

I did.

My Southside primary school was divided in two. Our early years were spent in the red building, a long, low red-brick construction with wings on either side of the central offices, a place that brings to mind milk in little glass bottles, learning to count with coloured wooden rods, making things with cardboard, raffia or wool, and Miss Anderson reading us stories. The grey building for the older pupils was built from stone. Tall and forbidding in appearance, it was a more conventional municipal school building. The first things, that it brings to mind, are the smell of nasty pink soap, being belted and Mr Samson.

It was in one of my first years at primary that one day a problem with staffing, never explained to us, arose, the effect of which was that my class, having no teacher, had to be transferred from the red building to the grey, to be supervised by one of the teachers there. This was alarming news to me and my tiny classmates. We lined up in twos holding hands and were marched away from the warmth and safety of our classroom up to the next playground, peopled by enormous and raucous youths, staring at our little column of infant interlopers. We looked up with dread as the sky was swallowed up by the grey monster, we were being ushered inside. The walls were tiled and on the many stairs we climbed, the bannisters were supported by iron bars. This was surely what prisons were like. Unlike our own familiar desks and chairs of plywood and tubular steel made to accommodate tiny children, this classroom contained ranks of hefty Victorian desks and chairs in one, constructed from cast iron and sloping dark wood, complete with ink wells. Behind his own desk, at the front of the class sat Mr Samson.

I had heard reports about Mr Samson. The back lanes of Strathbungo where we played football, French cricket and cops and robbers were also the places where we learned something about the wider world and its scary ways. This is where I was first told what sex was. I didn't actually believe it at the time; what was described seemed impractical and probably impossible. (To be honest, it still seems slightly improbable to me.) I learned that other families were not all like my own. Some children had less than happy homes and lives in which there was different food, sickness and even violence. While I suspected this was true, I chose to act in such a way that it wasn't. Older boys in the gang and those with older brothers and sisters told horror stories from school about how the work was hard, hours of homework had to be completed and punishment exercises were issued to wrongdoers. Then there was the belt. Before the European Court of Human Rights got involved, errant Scottish children were called to the front of the class and instructed to hold their shaking hands out in front of them. A thick leather belt split at the ends, specially manufactured for the purpose, was whipped down with some force onto soft young hands up to six times, causing swelling and bruising and of course extreme pain. This definitely couldn't be true. Could it? When stories about the belt were told they were usually associated with Mr Samson's name.

And there he was. He seemed immensely tall, with a receding hairline and a face cut from stone, but then a bit of perspective has to be considered on that. His grey suit sagged about him, its pockets bulging. What could be in them? As we shuffled and negotiated to find places, he already seemed impatient and irritable. Our class would have been an unwelcome imposition. His calls for quiet initially caused shock and fright. Miss Anderson didn't sound like this at all. Miss Anderson was a gentle soul who spoke softly and never gave the impression of annoyance or impatience. We missed Miss Anderson. As we hastened to assemble books and jotters and begin the prescribed work, he had clearly been instructed to set us, he looked on with his hands in his jacket pockets, giving the impression of clenched fists, or maybe he was clutching his belt. An uneasy lull settled on the class and we did our best to work away, too scared to ask questions, speak to each other or too frequently or too obviously to look up from our books. The sounds of coughing, pages being turned and seats being moved, produced a sequence of tutting, slamming down of his own papers and then sharp demands for silence. Eventually, a sustained period of relative quiet began, but at the slightest breath or murmur, I saw the mounting frustration on Mr Samson's face. I returned to my jotter. I reached for my pencil. Then it happened. I squirmed in agony as I saw and heard my hexagonal 2HB betrayer roll thunderously down the slope of my desk.

'Who was that?' he bellowed.

I froze. I pulled my grey school jumper down over the guilty pencil in my lap, not daring to look at my classmates.

'Who was it? Who did that? Stand up now!'

I didn't even try to understand why my crime was so heinous. I only knew that I was scared and wouldn't dream of owning up to it, to put myself in line for punishment by this furious and frightening man.

'In not admitting what you have done, one of you is lying. One of you is lying to me, lying to the class. You are not only telling a lie; you are acting a lie.'

Long minutes went by. He paced the room, glaring into small scared faces. I think one girl was crying softly behind me. I was not about to turn around. Eventually, he returned to his desk with this.

'I want the liar amongst you to remember what you have done today, in telling a lie, in acting a lie. Remember this with shame.'

The day crept towards a close and we were released. Never was the bell so shockingly loud, so welcome. The next day Miss Anderson was again in her place and slightly taken aback by the emotional state of her charges. One boy ran across the room to hug her knees.

In time our class moved up, progressing through classrooms, presided over by other teachers and on to the grey building, inevitably at last to become Mr Samson's class. By that time, we were a little more able to weather his moods, his temper, his outbursts. The fear had diminished but not disappeared. Along with many others, he belted me many times. Not for any criminality, violence or extreme behaviour, but for mucking about, having a laugh or speaking at the wrong time. I began to realise that his manner, the way he behaved, his anger and uneven treatment of us, seldom had much to do with us personally or how we behaved but things, events or histories beyond our knowledge or understanding. I sometimes wondered what was going on in his own life. Was there something hidden in him, something that he would be reluctant to admit to? Should I feel sorry for him?

I did remember what I had done that day, as he said, and it haunted me. The guilt, and yes shame, had lingered with me for a long time afterwards and while it did not take me long to settle in my mind that my crime was not a terrible one, the incident shook my sense of self. Was I a liar? Was I a coward, the sort of person who is unwilling or unable to accept responsibility? As a small boy, still uncertain about who I was and what my life would be, I found myself knocked off a previously happy course, shrinking within myself. I despised him for how he had made us feel, how he had made me feel. I wasn't going to forget Mr Samson.

I handed the letter to my wife, who read aloud tributes to a life 'devoted to the education and wellbeing of the countless children, who have thrived and prospered in his care, his first thought always for the child.'

'What should I wear?' she said.

'We're not going,' I said, crumpling the letter and throwing it into the bin.

And there it was again, that eyebrow, when I said, 'He's acting a lie.'

250 Battlefield Road by Christina Milarvie Quarrell

slow walking
is my joy
as I pass the Indian restaurant
battlefield road

memories rush in
music laughter dance
when young
this spot was our cafe
The Tiki

besotted by Tamla Motown
The Impressions
Four Tops
The Temptations
Junior Walker
our troop walked to and from
Gorbals and Govanhill
for the juke box therein

Big Rad(great dancer)
leading the way
walking home
we sang "ain't too proud to beg"
with all the moves

happy days
music still plays in my head

MAYFAIR MAYHEM by V McKenna

Some of you readers (those of you who are old enough) may have been present at the event remembered here. This is an account of it told to me by one, who personally participated in the mayhem at the Mayfair cinema, way back in 1973. The teller of the tale is a friend of mine but he prefers to remain anonymous. I bumped into this old friend last week, in front of what was once the well-kept garden of his family home -- now a vacant lot in Sinclair Drive on the Southside of Glasgow. We chatted, and he asked me if I remembered the old movie theatre, that once existed across the road. When I replied that I was too young to remember it, my friend fell into reminiscing.....

"In 1973, I was a schoolboy in my teens and my family home was just opposite the Mayfair cinema, here in Sinclair Drive, so I became an avid film fan. My pals and I were often to be found piling into the Mayfair, keen to view the latest film releases and it must be said, also keen to muck about and no doubt annoy those who had come to watch a movie." He smiled nostalgically thinking back...

"Cinemas in the 1970s were not the glossy, airconditioned, multi-screened places we see today. The Mayfair Picture house was run on a shoestring budget, with threadbare seats, wooden floors and a small, single screen. It had seating for maybe around a thousand people, and after purchasing your cinema ticket and your Butterkist popcorn from the booth in the foyer, you had to be quick off the mark to get to where you wanted to sit, as all seating was unreserved. You could either proceed to the stalls downstairs or climb the stairs to the balcony. My friends and I favoured the stalls usually, although on this particular occasion, we had a very specific reason to choose balcony seating. I was hooked. What was this "particular occasion" my friend remembered? His eyes were misty with recalling the past as he continued.

"In June 1973, the news broke that the Mayfair was going to close for good, and without question, this was a bitter blow to many of us, young and old residents of Southside Glasgow. This area, in the early 1970s, was pretty much devoid of entertainment for teenagers, unlike present times when young people have umpteen choices of things to do, but usually revert to communicating with each other on their digital devices." He frowned momentarily "Do I sound like a grumpy old man?" I made a non-committal noise and let him go on with the tale.

"I remember that the date for the closure of the cinema was announced as the last day of June, and at the same time it was revealed that the final film to be shown, on that final day, would be Soldier Blue. You might have heard of it. It's often described as one of the most traumatic and violent films ever made and the battle scenes were incredibly graphic and upsetting. Basically, the movie told the real life story of the infamous 1864 Sand Creek massacre in Colorado by the U.S. Cavalry on a Cheyenne Indian village and the events that led up to it." He paused to see if I fully grasped how violent the movie was. "The film climaxes with a horrific massacre, involving scenes of bloodshed, that even today, by our perhaps more desensitised standards, makes for very difficult viewing. And for your information, the film has often been seen as an allegory for the then Vietnam war." I felt the old man was about to go off at a tangent, and asked him to get back to the story of the cinema closure. He apologised and got back on track.

"When we heard that the closure of the Mayfair was to be coupled with the showing of this somewhat controversial movie, our first thought was that this presented an ideal opportunity for a prank of unparalleled proportions. We already knew of the film's reputation for harrowing and brutal scenes, and so we decided to create a prank, in line with the horrific events of the film's climax. In this way, no one would forget either the movie or the last day in the life of the venue. That was the plan." His voice shook slightly with excitement as he revealed all that had taken place across the road, fifty years ago.

"So it was, that on the last night of the cinema, seven teenage lads, myself included, advanced upon the Mayfair with suspiciously bulging jackets. Forgoing the Butterkist on offer in the ticket office, our group hurried upstairs to grab seats in the front row of the balcony. Then, as soon as the lights dimmed and wee Frank, the usher had gone downstairs, we unbuttoned our jackets to reveal their contents –newspapers. Next, one of our group pulled a suit jacket and trousers out of his backpack along with a football, and as soon as the familiar strains of the Pearl and Dean music started up, the front row became a hive of activity as we began furiously scrunching up the sheets of newspaper. Fortunately, the then familiar "pa pa papa" advertising tune drowned out our noisy activity --the first stage of our project. We tried keeping quiet, but mirth overtook us and at some point, the usher notified of our noisy behaviour, shone a torch onto us and we momentarily froze, but as soon as he disappeared downstairs, the scrunching continued. Finally, we had created a large enough pile of scrunched-up paper and then stage two of the plan was initiated –the stuffing of the suit. Eventually, triumphantly, our hard work was done and a fully stuffed dummy, with a football for a head, was given a seat alongside us seven pals." We both chuckled at the incongruous picture my friend painted and then he went on.

"For the eight of us, up in the balcony, the tension mounted throughout the showing of the rest of the film. The plan had been well sorted in advance --once the movie reached its climatic and gruesome last scenes, where bodies were being scattered about on screen, the idea was to throw the dummy from the balcony. It would fall onto the empty seats below thus mirroring the horrific ending of the movie and giving all the downstairs audience a fright. And it would be an event to stay, hopefully, in the memories of all those fans of the Mayfair cinema.

At last, the final scene arrived and as bodies started flying about on screen, with an appropriately blood-curdling scream, the dummy was cast over the side of the balcony onto the seats below. As the mannequin fell and then sprawled in a life-like fashion across the empty seats, the audience was unsurprisingly very surprised. I remember there were two local policemen attending at the back of the theatre and they rushed forward to handle the horror, as some members of the audience screamed in fright. Others, no doubt guessing that they were witnessing a prank and somewhat annoyed at the interruption understandably, jeered and booed. By now, though the film credits were rolling on screen and we, satisfied that the event was complete, abandoned the dummy and fled the scene." Now, out of breath from the long telling of his tale, my friend seemed to deflate, and indicating with his walking stick the empty grounds, where once his family home stood, he finished his story.

"I recall that the next day I came out of my house, that once stood here, and looking over at the Mayfair I spotted the dummy, abandoned on the steps of the now closed down cinema. I remember I gave him a wave and then nonchalantly whistling, I walked on by." At this, my friend gave me a wave and quietly whistling, he hobbled away. As he disappeared into the library, I imagined I heard the screams, as the dummy was hurled over the balcony, and in my mind's eye, clearly saw those young men, full of youthful stupidity, enjoying that last night fifty years ago, creating mayhem at the Mayfair.

Corporal Edward Ferrie by Tracey McBain

Edward, Eddie or was it little Ed,
Too young, too sweet, to surely be dead?
The telegram - 'Killed in Action, Dardanelles'
Felled by thundering, tumbling, blood-stained shells.

A son, a brother, a good friend too,
You were the uncle we never knew.
June 28th – the halt to your chime
Who could you have been given more time?

The moment of truth, an unwanted blow
A family in retreat, moving too slow.
The news a loved one will never return,
An unending battle, with no about-turn.

Your voice I imagine, full of bravado,
Accented, teenage, now incommunicado.
Your face, blurred, through eyes that mist,
A sad lament for girls never kissed.

Toy soldiers united one and all
Many destined to tragically fall
Taking your place in our own history
A central character, a tragic mystery.

100 years later, at the end of this time
Some now ask 'was this a crime'?
And what to say – the dead are still dead
All those Edwards, Eddies and sweet little Eds.

FAME AND MUSIC by Willie Brown

When John, Matt, Denis and Pat formed Simply Devine in 1979, they soon discovered the benefits of being in a band. They became instantly popular with their peers, particularly the girls.

Their long-term ambition was to win a recording contract and have a hit record, but for now, they settled for being the pre-disco entertainment at the sixth-year graduation ball, a glitzy event held in Shawlands Academy School Hall. They were very excited to be asked to do this, their first public engagement, even if it was for free. This first short concert helped hone their skills in stagecraft, as they wowed the audience with cover versions of rock anthems.

Other gigs followed and the boys built a reputation for playing solid rock music. It was time to get themselves a manager. That turned out to be Pat's Dad - who to be fair was able to procure gigs in pubs and clubs in Glasgow's Southside. Local venues like the Doune Castle, the Shawlands Hotel, the Mulberry Hotel and The Shaws Bar. They played whatever the punters wanted to hear - covers of well-known songs. They were happy to do this as they continued to improve as musicians. Their next big break came when the band secured a residency in the Newlands Hotel (JJ Booths) on Sunday nights. They were working in a culture of heavy alcohol consumption and smoke inhalation but they were getting a lot of attention from the girls, a utopia for boys in their late teens.

However, after enjoying the fruits of their popularity for a few months, the band were beginning to get frustrated at the type of music they were being asked to play. They wanted to evolve, and that meant writing and performing their own songs. Unfortunately, any time an original song was announced, the disapproval of the audience was quite palpable. The crowd only wanted to hear the same old, same old tunes. It was getting boring.

The band were also becoming frustrated that there was still no sign of a recording contract, despite having sent out hundreds of demo tapes. Was it time to give up on the dream?

Over the next couple of years, the guys began to settle down with wives and girlfriends, and in Matt's case, with children. They sort of settled for that and the group evolved into a tribute band. They toured Central Scotland venues, adding a female singer called Gail to the group, performing as Fleetwood Sixpack for the first half of their act, before Matt took over for the second half, as he morphed into Neil Diamond. They were very popular but their creative skills were thwarted as no one wanted to hear their songs. They got to the stage where they hated "Sweet Caroline".

Then, out of the blue, a representative from TOPIC Records contacted them offering a one-album, one-single deal. The boys decided to accept. With no other offers on the table, it was the only chance they would ever get to make the big time. It really was a no-brainer.

The project took about a year to complete and the album was released, alongside a single. The company, in fairness, spent a lot of money promoting the product and touting the records to all the major stations. It worked. Success at last, as Radio 1's Steve Wright, selected their single as his record of the week. The single was called "Rock This World".

Despite this newfound success, the boys in the band were not happy. They felt they had no control over the songs on their album or the one chosen as a single. They had submitted over 40 songs with their preferences at the top. They wanted to be known as serious rock musicians but the recording company wanted them to be a mature boy band. The guys collectively decided to keep schtum and go with the flow. For the first time, the band had made some real money from music. The boys had all left their day jobs in the hope of making the big time, despite not being fully on board with their lack of input and decision-making. They decided to accept whatever advice they were given, for the time being.

The single entered the charts at Number 36 and climbed to Number 15. They were getting noticed and reviewed by the musical press and TV companies and were lined up to appear on Top of the Pops. This was all arranged via the recording company, without consultation with the band who were becoming peeved at some of the things they were asked to do.

When they arrived at the studios, hours before the recording, the band were greeted by the stylist, the make-up artist, the costume adviser and the rest of the image-making crew. They were all separated to an allocated adviser and passed around like pieces of meat. They were uneasy because all the arrangements had been made by the recording company, who had already forced them to eject Gail from the band as it did not fit with their image. Individually no one was happy and they decided that after the recording they would have a band "meet".

The recording took place after the guys had been groomed, poked, prodded and polished. They were shell-shocked.

"How was it for you John?" Matt asked tentatively, (thinking he had heard a kerfuffle coming from the room John was in).

"I can't believe what I let happen to me. Destiny told me I was too hirsute for TV and offered to wax my back, sac and crack. I just told her, no way. Who's gonnae look at my back, sac and crack? So I said no-then okay. She said drummers went topless. I said I don't - not with my scar tissue issue! What about you Matt?" John rasped.

"Fuck! I got told, pity I was married, but could I pretend my kids were called Rocket and Sky for the image. I told that Reggie where to go."

Denis said "I was told by Tulisa I would look heavier on TV. She said they could wrap me up in cling film as a stop-gap, until my weight loss training plan was designed. Cheeky bastard. I told her I couldn't give a monkeys how I looked on TV. She just glared back. I let her put the cling film on - I am roasting."

Pat was last to say anything. "I was told to dye my hair blonde and shave off my mouser if I wanted to fit in with the group's image. I mean, could you imagine me without my mouser? I'm a modern-day Rabbie Burns. Look guys, I really, really don't like the limelight. I'm out, jumping off this carousel before it kills me."

"Look this fame thing is not for us," John announced. "I think we should all jump ship."

The contract was torn up in the quickest-ever dissolution of a band. The group would be consigned to the one-hit-wonder box forever but they didn't care. Everyone went back to their day jobs.

Forty years later, Denis is still a funeral director, John a retired electrician and Pat a joiner. Only Matt the singer has stayed in showbiz, as a part-time Michael Buble tribute act. He sells fruit and veg during the day. They are all happy people who realized they would never fit into the world of pop culture. They were famous for 5 minutes.

The Granary, 1985 by Deborah Portilla

The Granary, known as a pub where the banter flows as freely as the drinks, was the place to be seen if you frequented Southside Glasgow in the eighties. If you were slightly less ostentatious, it was a great place to people watch. The one thing I remember vividly about Friday nights there, was the overwhelming number of leggy blondes. Huge, big volume styled blondes were everywhere. I was a short brunette. I could never get served at the bar, overlooked by the longer of limb and fairer of hair females dwarfing me. And then add on the shoulder pads… You could see the girls coming from a mile down Kilmarnock Road.

I just watched the Andrew McCarthy documentary Brats tonight which covers the same period of time in the eighties. It looks back on the interview by the New York magazine writer, David Blum, who coined the phrase 'Bratpack'. He essentially wrote a profile of Emilio Estevez and included several up and coming actors like McCarthy, Rob Lowe, Demi Moore and Molly Ringwald – basically the cast of The Breakfast Club. Bratpack members were crucially wider than the one film though, and included actors Tom Cruise, Sean Penn and Timothy Hutton.

The documentary follows McCarthy examining how the tag affected him at the time. Did it affect his career? Did he let it affect his life? He then goes in search of some of the others and talks to them about their memories of that time. Some seem very nonchalant about it all, particularly Rob Lowe, who seemed unaffected by the Bratpack tag. Others, like Demi

Moore, had obviously struggled. In her conversation with Andrew, it was obvious that she had been through so much therapy to get to a place where she was comfortable.

Now you may think it's quite a stretch to go from Shawlands in 1985 to the Bratpack, but when I think back the vibes were similar.

The Granary regulars were in their twenties, on the cusp of beginning the rest of their lives. Optimism and confidence filled the bar. A fair amount of bullshit pervaded the Southside air, make no mistake. It was a time before life's trials and commitments hit hard. No mortgages, marriages or kids. Who knew what lay in the future?

So what better to do on a Friday night in Southside Glasgow? Dig out your shoulder pads and head for your local. There's plenty of time to worry about the rest of your life. Revel in the best Southside has to offer. Welcome to The Granary in 1985.

Yawn Bonnie Banks by Barney MacFarlane

HOW tiresome: Dougie regarded his mirror image – not so flash now. Released five years early from a 20 stretch, jails needed space for race rioters. His class of prisoner, the bank robber – an elite few – were on the wane.

So, what now? Only one bank remained in his neck of Glasgow's South Side. And that probably didn't carry much cash, everyone banking online.

Reminisced with old colleague, Swift Charlie, in a pub ... yes, there were still pubs, though they sold coffee and snacks as well.

"You've been away too long," said Charlie. "Of course, you got a few years added for blasting that teller trying to press the alarm."

"Aye, but I only disfigured her," moaned Dougie. "Ten years extra for nothin'. "

"And nae banks left tae rob."

Charlie stared at his pal. "Cryptocurrency's the thing. Saw a story the other day about a guy made a few bob stealing bitcoin." Adding, "Tech genius, mind you. A wee bit here, a wee bit there."

"Ach, don't bank on it", said Dougie, forlorn.

Full Circle by Rosalyn Barclay

Julie stopped in her tracks, thinking she recognised the man who had just walked past her in the street.

"Was that Stephen?" she asked herself. They had gone out during their last year at school and for a year after. Until he disappeared one day, that is. She turned around, but the man quickly hurried away. If it was Stephen he didn't want to talk.

His had been a troubled upbringing. His father was an alcoholic, who worked in the building trade and often got sent home or sacked for turning up hungover and smelling of alcohol. Matters came to a head one day and his Mum told Stephen to pack a suitcase. "We're leaving now, before Dad gets home. It's the summer holidays and I can get you into a new school before the term starts."

"Why?" Stephen asked in tears. "I'll miss my friends."

"Just hurry up and pack what you need. A taxi is coming in half an hour. We're going to a place where your dad won't find us."

Stephen ran into his bedroom and grabbed what clothes and things he thought he should take.

"I'm ready," he said as his mum furiously packed what she needed. She rummaged through her kitchen cupboards and wardrobes, quickly filling up two suitcases and was ready when the taxi arrived. Marian, left a terse note for her husband. "Gone, I've had enough."

Mother and son got into the taxi and headed to Glasgow Women's Aid, where Marian had contacted earlier. Stephen was still in tears. She tried to console her son but she too was worried about the future. One day at a time she decided.

They were moving to the opposite end of the city, from the north to the southside. Marian's priority was finding a new home and a school for Stephen. With the help of her support worker, she started looking for a small flat that she could afford. She was lucky to find one near a high school that Stephen could attend. She had heard good things about this school.

Marian's job had been in the library near her old house but she had managed to arrange a transfer to one in the southside. Now she worried that her husband might try to find her by looking in libraries across the city.

Stephen didn't fit in well at his new school. Teenage hormones caused fluctuations in his moods; one minute happy, the next grumpy. He found it difficult to make friends and became a bit of a loner. His saving grace was that he was good with computers.

There was a lot of bullying going on, and Stephen was one of the victims. He felt he received no help from anyone. His mother had struggles of her own, trying to make ends meet and they had no contact with other family members. There were no male relatives that Steven could turn to for advice. Marian tried to reassure her son that all would be well, and that it takes time to settle into a new school.

After a couple of years, Stephen did settle down at school. He met Julie at a school disco and thought he had met the love of his life. Despite his troubled background, he worked and studied hard. Enough to pass his Higher exams and obtain a place at university. He didn't however feel it was the right time for him to go into higher education. Instead, he found a job in a call centre, which suited him as there was no face-to-face contact with people. Just being a voice on the phone worked for him. After only a few months he was offered a promotion, but it meant moving to Wales. For Stephen, it was only going to be a stopgap, as he had plans in his head to work for himself. He left abruptly and didn't tell Julie

Stephen found a compact second-floor apartment near his new office. It was in a modern block, just big enough for him. It had one bedroom and a cosy sitting room with a kitchen in the corner. The new job entailed nothing more than selling gas and electricity plans to customers over the phone. It was not too taxing which allowed Steven time to think about what kind of business he might set up.

The town had a number of antique/second-hand shops and Stephen started to frequent them in his spare time. He thought he could buy things in these shops and sell them on internet auction sites. There were lots of leather goods for sale, so prices were low. Steven decided this should be his first purchase.

Stephen approached the owner in one of the shops. "I'm looking for a nice bag for my girlfriend, quite small, just for evenings out. You know the kind girls like, small but big enough for their lipstick, brush and purse."

"We have plenty of them. Which colour would she prefer?"

"Oh, black."

The owner collected together a selection of black bags. Steven picked the one he thought would make the greatest profit online. Back home he got to work selling the bag. He didn't make much money on that first sale, but it was a start. His next step was to try selling jewellery and see if that worked out better.

In another shop, Stephen went through the same routine. "I'm looking for some jewellery for my girlfriend's birthday."

"What had you in mind?"

"A necklace and earrings. In gold please," he replied.

"I'll see what I've got."

Stephen surveyed the shop while he waited and was sure he saw someone he had gone to secondary school with. "Surely, it can't be," he thought. "I am here to escape from Glasgow and come across someone I know." When the owner brought over some pieces, Stephen quickly picked something and got out of the shop. On the way back to the flat he was not thinking about selling jewellery, he was thinking about home, his mum and Julie. The jewellery he had bought was sold at a loss and Steven gave up on the idea of internet selling.

A few weeks later, Stephen went out to buy some food, and of all people, he bumped into Colin, the guy from the shop.

"It's Stephen, isn't it? What are you doing down here?"

"I've got a job here. What about you?"

"I had to get away from Glasgow. It was constant trouble, I needed a complete change."

Stephen laughed. "Yeah, I wanted a change too but now I'm not so sure it was the right move. I left my girlfriend in the lurch, which I feel bad about and I miss my mum. I've been thinking of moving back to Scotland and applying again to university. Maybe become a computer studies teacher."

"Good God!" Colin exclaimed. "You could go full circle and end up back teaching at our old school. Now that would be something because I remember you getting a hard time from some people"

"You're reading my mind, Colin. That's what I was thinking of."

Stephen stuck out the job at the call centre for another six months. When his university application was successful, he gave up his flat and returned to Glasgow, to his mother's delight.

"I am so glad to have you back son," she said, hugging him. "Wales was just so far away. I don't know why you moved there."

"Neither do I, Mum," he said laughing. "I needed a change, but I am back now, and I am going to be a teacher."

Stephen enrolled at Glasgow University and he loved it, becoming a diligent student, which he probably wouldn't have been if he had gone straight there from school. After four years of study, he trained as a teacher in Computer Science and Maths. Steven was thrilled to land a one-year probationary job at his old high school and particularly enjoyed helping pupils who were struggling.

Stephen excelled in his probation year and was offered a permanent job. He always looked out for pupils who seemed to be loners, remembering what it felt like when he was at school himself.

There was a further bonus. Julie, whom he'd left abruptly, was also at the school as a language teacher. He didn't ignore her this time and they resumed their friendship, which rapidly turned into a renewed relationship.

Despite his adverse and troubled background, Stephen was a popular and successful teacher and he and Julie married a few years later. His life, as Colin had predicted back in Wales, had come full circle.

Ode to the Cairns by Stephen Tiggerdine

Tall and stony they stand
Defying the wind and the rain,
A principled symbol of all that was lost,
Of hearts that stayed strong no matter the cost
Tall and stony they stand

Moody and silent they stand,
cold aspects of permanent pain.
A forlorn reminder to one and all
Of what's to be gained in righteous downfall,
Moody and silent they stand

Ignoring the world they stand,
While visitors gaze in disdain.
Knowing little of Charlie, the clans or Loch Shiel,
Or how such great leaders caused proud men to feel,
Ignored by the world they stand

Unique in my memory they stand
In my grief-stricken mind like a stain;
To Culloden I journeyed from old Kennishead,
A Southsider weeping for warriors long dead
Unique in my memory they stand.

Comparison-ready they stand,
Our perspectives being never the same
The Burrell Collection appealing to me,
Those far-travelled relics much gentler to see
Comparison-ready they stand.

Composed after a visit to Culloden battlefield and the Glenfinnan monument.

Other books from Battlefield Writers

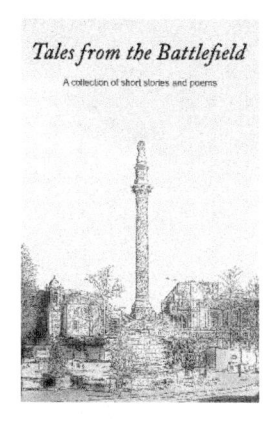

Tales from the Battlefield

Beyond the Battlefield

For books by individual writers visit
www.battlefieldwriters.com

Printed in Great Britain
by Amazon